UNDONE BY THE SULTAN'S TOUCH

Khaled ~~a~~ze her ~~f~~ ~~t~~he
~~p~~ ~~sie would finally~~

finally be his in every possible way.

That same fire she'd tasted that night three months ago simmered in her at the thought, making her cheeks heat, making her stomach clench in delicious anticipation, making her feel hungry and wild despite all the eyes trained on her.

Almost as if he'd left them both unfulfilled deliberately.

"Where are we going?" she asked when Khaled finally took her by the hand and led her from the banquet to the sound of many cheers, though the truth was she didn't care at all as long as he was with her.

"You will see when we get there," Khaled told her, and then he smiled down at her in a way that made her quiver deep inside, all that dark intent on his fierce face, all of his focus on her at last. *At last.* "Though I must warn you, *wife,* that I doubt you will see much at all outside my bed."

Caitlin Crews discovered her first romance novel at the age of twelve. It involved swashbuckling pirates, grand adventures, a heroine with rustling skirts and a mind of her own, and a seriously mouth-watering and masterful hero. The book (the title of which remains lost in the mists of time) made a serious impression. Caitlin was immediately smitten with romances and romance heroes, to the detriment of her middle school social life. And so began her lifelong love affair with romance novels, many of which she insists on keeping near her at all times.

Caitlin has made her home in places as far-flung as York, England, and Atlanta, Georgia. She was raised near New York City, and fell in love with London on her first visit when she was a teenager. She has backpacked in Zimbabwe, been on safari in Botswana, and visited tiny villages in Namibia. She has, while visiting the place in question, declared her intention to live in Prague, Dublin, Paris, Athens, Nice, the Greek Islands, Rome, Venice, and/or any of the Hawaiian islands. Writing about exotic places seems like the next best thing to moving there.

She currently lives in California, with her animator/comic book artist husband and their menagerie of ridiculous animals.

Recent titles by the same author:

A SCANDAL IN THE HEADLINES
  (Sicily's Corretti Dynasty)
A ROYAL WITHOUT RULES (Royal & Ruthless)
NO MORE SWEET SURRENDER
  (Scandal in the Spotlight)
A DEVIL IN DISGUISE

CHAPTER ONE

THE GIRL CAME out of nowhere.

Cleo Churchill stamped on the brakes in her tiny rental car, gasping as the car swerved before coming to a jolting halt in the narrow little alley of a road somewhere deep in the twisting, ancient heart of the capital city of Jhurat.

For one panicked heartbeat, then another, she thought she'd been seeing things. The blazing desert sun was only then beginning to drop behind the ornate historic buildings, making the shadows lengthen and stretch. She'd lost her way in the tangle of old streets and one city looked very much like another after six months of traveling all around Europe and into the Middle East. And more to the point, there was absolutely no reason a girl should *dive* in front of her car—

But there she was, young and wide-eyed and startlingly pretty behind her flowing scarves, right there at the passenger window—seemingly unharmed.

I didn't hit her, thank God.

"Please!" The girl spoke through the car's open window, desperate and direct. "Help me!"

Cleo didn't think. The adrenaline of the near miss hummed through her with an almost sickening electricity, but she motioned toward the door, aware as she did it that her hands were shaking.

"Are you all right?" she asked as the girl wrenched

open the door and threw herself inside. "Are you hurt? Do you need—?"

"Drive!" the girl cried as if pursued by demons. "Please! Before—"

Cleo didn't wait to find out *before what*. She'd escaped her own demons, hadn't she? She knew how it was done. She stepped on the gas pedal, scowling as she concentrated fiercely on the narrow road in front of her, which she dearly hoped led back out of this maze of ancient narrow streets that wound erratically around Jhurat's central palace, home to its governing sultan. Beside her, the girl breathed heavily and high-pitched, as if she'd been running.

"You're okay," Cleo said, trying to soothe her—or even herself. "We're okay now."

And then a man stalked out of the shadows, directly into the car's path, as if daring Cleo to run straight into him. She heard herself gasp out a curse, but her eyes were fixed on him as surely as if he'd demanded it.

He was tall and fierce, forbidding and uncompromising in the loose robes that marked him a local—a wealthy local—and did nothing at all to conceal his markedly powerful form. The sun was behind him and hid his face, but Cleo could still *feel* the weight of his stare. Like an impossible knot in her own chest.

He stood there in the center of the road, imperious and bold. He crossed his arms over his broad chest and waited—and it wasn't until she realized he wasn't moving that she also realized she wasn't, either. That she'd stopped the car directly in front of him as if he'd held up his hands like a police officer and commanded it.

When all he'd done was stare.

Despite herself, Cleo shivered. Foreboding. Fear.

And something else, maybe, beneath it, that she'd never felt before.

He bit out something ferocious in Arabic that made the

girl beside her jerk in her seat as if he'd slapped her, and Cleo's stomach twisted.

This is not good, she thought.

"Get out of the car," he said then, his voice deep and autocratic, and it took a long, shuddering moment for Cleo to realize that this time, he was speaking directly to her. Issuing an implacable order in a language she could understand, right through the glass. "Now."

"Who is that?" she whispered, still unable to pull her gaze away from him. He was simply too mesmerizing. Too powerful.

The girl beside her let out a sound that was something like a sob, but far angrier. When Cleo finally managed to yank her attention away from the dark and dangerous man taking over the road before them, the girl's jaw was set in a stubborn line, and her mouth trembled. Making her look even younger than Cleo had originally thought she was.

"That," the girl said bitterly, staring out the front window at the man who still stood there, not moving an inch, as if he expected it to be nothing but a matter of moments before he was obeyed, "is His Excellency, the Sultan of Jhurat."

This was, Cleo realized dimly then, a great deal worse than *not good.*

"What?" she asked weakly, that thudding panic hitting harder, sending out shock waves. He didn't look like a sultan. He looked like some kind of warrior angel, sent down to smite and awe. She felt both smitten and awed, the sensations too hot and almost painful inside of her. "Why would a sultan—*the* sultan—chase you down an alley?"

"Because he is a demon from hell." The girl's mouth twisted. "He is also my brother."

Cleo swallowed, hard.

He stood there, waiting. And now she understood what that proud ruthlessness meant. What that *thing* was that emanated from him like a force field, rendering the whole city small and inconsequential beside him.

Cleo's mind raced, and for some reason, she thought of Brian then. Weak, lying Brian. Brian, who had humiliated her. Brian, who had said he loved her but couldn't possibly have meant it, could he? Brian, who she'd believed so completely when he'd never had even a shred of the intensity or authority the man before her simply...*oozed*.

The sultan jerked his head in a silent yet remarkably eloquent command to exit the vehicle.

Immediately.

And Cleo forgot about stupid, cheating Brian and the girlfriend he'd kept on the side for almost the entirety of their doomed engagement.

This was exactly the kind of thing she'd promised her parents back in Ohio would never happen to her, because she'd imagined she was too smart, or too cynical, to fall prey to scenarios like this. This was exactly what her mother and her hysterical aunts had predicted would happen if she did something so radical as explore the world by herself. She could practically *hear* the doom-and-gloom predictions they'd all shared with her whether she'd wanted them to or not, like a going-away present, as if they were whispering it in her ear from across the planet.

They'd begged her not to do this. They'd told her running away from her problems was only running straight into new ones. And now look what had happened.

The sultan waited. Less patient by the moment.

"Just drive over him," the girl beside her demanded. "Mow him down where he stands."

"I can't," Cleo said, except she found she was whispering. "I can't do that."

And everything seemed to slow down, as though the air was made of syrup and there was nothing but him. That man. *The sultan*. She shifted the car into Park. Beside her, the girl let out a frustrated noise, but Cleo's attention was riveted on the man at the end of her bumper.

Still. Watchful. Ferocious.

Her neck prickled with a deep foreboding. With anxiety. With the sense of immensity, as if what she was about to do was already sealed in stone, as ancient and unmoving and inevitable as the venerable city around her, as the old streets beneath her.

As the man before her. The sultan of all he surveyed.

Who couldn't be weak, she knew somehow, if he tried.

Cleo turned off the rental car's ignition with a decisive click and then opened her door, ignoring the girl in the passenger seat as she got out and stood there.

The sultan moved then. He nodded at someone behind her and men in military uniforms appeared as if from thin air, surrounding the rental car, all wearing machine guns that dwarfed their bodies.

Cleo didn't understand a single word of the rapid-fire Arabic, all shouted back and forth in so many harsh and loud male voices, and yet somehow she couldn't bring herself to look away from the sultan as he continued to stand there staring back at her.

One of his men appeared beside her and held out his hand, making Cleo flinch. She glanced at him, then back at the sultan, aware then of how fragile she was. She felt it in ways she never had before. Fragile and exposed and frighteningly vulnerable.

And it was still better than how Brian had made her feel, two weeks before their wedding, when she'd come home early from work and found him on the living room floor of his condo with that woman.

The sultan said something, and she realized it wasn't the first time.

"I'm sorry, I didn't hear you," she said, and she hardly sounded like herself.

He paused, and she wished she had something more than this shadowy impression of his face. That the sun would hide behind the buildings at last so she could look at him without her eyes watering. So she could convince herself that he was neither as cruel nor as inhuman as he appeared while backlit like a god.

So she could tell herself that the twisting heat that knotted her belly, low and hot, was based on something more than the intuition she'd learned better than to trust.

But his voice, when it came, was as calm as it was deep, despite the tension she could hear beneath it, and for no reason at all, it eased her. Even as it set her on fire.

"Do you know who I am?"

"Yes."

A faint nod. "Give my man your keys."

An implacable order delivered in perfect English, with a crisp British accent to boot. Cleo knew she should ask questions. Demand to know what was happening to her, what he planned to do next. Instead, she simply obeyed.

She opened her hand and the man beside her took the keys from her palm, and the whole time she was lost in the will of the powerful man whose face was still in shadows before her.

Why couldn't she seem to breathe? Why did it feel as if the earth were buckling beneath her feet when she could see—because no one else was reacting to it, no one else was moving, the car was solid and unmoving beside her—that it was only happening inside of her?

Everything seemed to stretch out, slow and taut, but then the car engine turned over beside her, the men and the car and the angry girl disappeared after a brief consultation, and Cleo was standing alone in an alleyway in a foreign country with a man so great and powerful he held a title she'd half believed only existed in books.

He moved then, and she wished he hadn't. He was like

liquid, a threat wrapped in poetry, athletic and menacing at once. The knot inside her pulled taut, red and hot. Cleo stood still as he walked in a slow circle around her. He held something in his hands and she realized it was the wallet she'd left sitting in one of the cup holders in the car. One of his men must have—

"Eyes on me," he ordered her, his voice a silken command.

And when she jerked her attention back up from her wallet to his face, she could see it, finally. Could see *him.*

Beautiful, something whispered inside her, though he wasn't.

He was much too fierce. He reminded her of those remote villages she'd found in her travels, clinging to the sides of rugged mountains long days from anywhere, proud and breathtaking and unimaginably tough. He had thick dark hair and a poet's face made shockingly masculine by a warrior's cool, light gaze and the sort of tough jaw Cleo associated with soldiers and martial artists—and thugs. A blade of a nose. Faint lines around his eyes suggested he must have smiled at some point in his life, but she couldn't imagine it. He seemed carved entirely from stone.

He looked so masculine and so inarguably fierce it was almost as if he and soft, round-faced, *nice-looking* Brian were of a different species. She told herself that was why her heart beat so fast. Because he was the *not Brian.*

And because he really was beautiful.

"You are American."

It wasn't a question.

"Yes."

His gaze moved over her and she had to fight not to squirm. She was wearing dark trousers and scuffed boots beneath a loose-fitting T-shirt, and a dark jacket as much to cover herself in this conservative part of the world as to block the faint chill in the air, hinting at the coming fall night. She'd twisted her long hair back, but the long day had coaxed some of it down again, strands falling forward messily and making her feel much younger than her twenty-five years.

Cleo didn't want to ask herself why, exactly, she wished there was something more in his dark gaze then. Something to match that heat inside her.

He flipped open her wallet and looked inside. "You are a very long way from Ohio."

"I'm traveling," she said, and her voice sounded strange. Huskier than usual. Raw, somehow. "Backpacking."

"Alone?"

She didn't want to admit that, for some reason. For a hundred reasons. But he lifted his gaze from her wallet and the license he was presumably studying, and she felt hot. Caught.

"Yes," she said, fighting to sound normal. "It's been six months. I fly home in two weeks."

And the truth was, she didn't want to go back. Not yet. Maybe not ever.

"Unless, of course, you find yourself detained," he said, as if he could read her mind.

She frowned. "Why would I find myself detained?"

"A prison sentence would be considered a lenient penalty in this country for a foreign national caught in the act of kidnapping a member of the sultan's family," he said, almost casually.

It was undoubtedly suicidal to scowl at this man. But Cleo only thought about that after she did it.

"I didn't kidnap anyone. Your sister ran in front of my car. Should I have flattened her beneath my tires?" She didn't remember herself so much as see that incredulous expression on his face, and she coughed once. Delicately. "I thought I was helping. And also not committing vehicular manslaughter."

The sultan stared at her for a moment, that incredulous expression shifting to something else. Something far more dangerous.

"What do you imagine my sister was running from?" he asked, and it occurred to her that his easy, casual tone was in truth neither of those things.

"Maybe you're marrying her off? To some ally or other?"

But that notion came from novels she'd read, not any particular knowledge about this place or him, and he seemed to know that. Even to expect it, she thought, when his slate-gray eyes darkened.

His magnificent mouth, already close to cruel in its beauty, thinned. He watched her for a moment, his cool gaze like a fire inside her, turning her inside out.

That had to be panic, she told herself, but she knew better.

"What a vivid imagination you have, Miss Churchill."

She didn't want him to know her name. She didn't want him to look at her like that, or at all. She wanted to run.

Except she really didn't. She'd been running for six months. This was the first time she'd wanted to stand still instead. Cleo couldn't let herself think too much about that. It made the heat in her burn hotter.

"Your sister didn't tell me what she was running from," she said, somehow sounding far cooler than she felt. And not because she couldn't seem to do anything but obey him, no matter if the order he gave her was silent, conveyed by those smoky gray eyes that she found as unnerving as she did mesmerizing. "She jumped in the car, that's all. And then you appeared before us like every horror-movie villain in the history of mankind. Only without an ax. Happily."

Again, that arrested look. That slow blink, as if he couldn't believe she'd said that. Neither could she.

"My sister is sixteen." His voice was low. Measured. "She doesn't wish to return to her boarding school. What you interrupted was a tantrum."

"She asked for my help," Cleo said staunchly, and found herself lifting up her chin in a defiance that had to mean she had some kind of death wish. "And I'm not going to apologize for helping her, no matter how ferocious you become."

He studied her, cold and fierce and impassive. *He is a sultan,* her brain kept reminding her. *This is deeply, deeply foolish.* He could do as he liked with her, and they both knew it. Mouthing off to a man like this had to be right up there in the top two dumbest things she'd ever done, right next to *trust Brian.*

"You are fortunate, I think, that I don't require your apologies," he told her, and yet the way he said it made her feel anything but *fortunate,* despite that glowing knot of heat low in her belly. "But I'm afraid you must come with me anyway."

Khaled bin Aziz, Sultan of Jhurat for the moment—assuming he could keep clinging to his country by his damned fingernails—stood outside the small private foyer in the old palace where his guards had sequestered the American girl, and considered his next move.

His sister had been taken to her rooms—where she would remain until morning, when his guards would personally transport her to her boarding school in the countryside and make sure her teachers there were prepared to monitor her movements more closely. He knew it wasn't Amira's fault that she acted this way, so heedless and irresponsible, kicking up the kind of trouble she couldn't possibly understand had far-reaching consequences.

Khaled could remember being sixteen and angry at everything himself, but, of course, he hadn't had the luxury of indulging either his youth or his temper. He'd been too busy bearing the brunt of his responsibilities as their father's heir.

You do not matter, his father had told him when he was barely eight and then with great regularity thereafter. *Only Jhurat matters. Accept this truth.*

Nor could Khaled indulge his own temper now. There was too much at stake. Trade negotiations with Western powers who took such pleasure in believing him a barbarian for the kind of commerce that Jhurat very much needed to secure if it was going to escape the curse of endless poverty that had afflicted so many of its neighbors, and had nearly crippled it, too, beneath the weight of his father's paranoia and attempts to alleviate his own guilt.

Open the borders and you open Pandora's box, his father had predicted balefully in one of his coherent moments, but it wasn't until now that Khaled had fully understood what he'd meant.

He didn't blame Amira, but he could kill her all the same for throwing him neck-deep into problems he wished someone else could solve. But that was what happened upon inheriting a country far earlier than expected after its ruler, his father, had collapsed and had been declared incompetent: there was no one else. These problems were Khaled's alone.

"She is no one of importance," his head of security, Nasser, said quietly from beside him, his gaze on the sleek computer tablet in his hands. "Her family is unremarkable. Her father is an electrician and her mother works in a doctor's office in a small town on the outskirts of what appears to be a very small city in the middle of the country. She has two sisters, one married to a mechanic and the other to a teacher. No ties to anyone with any sort of influence at all."

"Ah," Khaled said, more to himself than Nasser, "but

that only means she is one of their 'every women.' I learned at Harvard that Americans love nothing more than to tell themselves fairy stories in which little brown mice become great and powerful through their own inner strength, or some such nonsense. It is part of their cultural DNA."

Inside the room, his own little brown mouse sat on one of the settees, bent over at the waist, elbows on her knees and her forehead cradled in her hands. He thought she was simply breathing deeply, not weeping. Not this one, with her talk of villains and axes and her foolish courage. He'd seen the hint of fear in her eyes when he'd ordered her back to the palace. He'd scared her, he knew, and if he regretted that—if he regretted the necessity of squelching that spark of defiant fire that had transformed her from a mouse into something far more interesting out in that alley, if he regretted the man he'd become that he could do these things so cavalierly—he ignored it.

There was no place for regret. There never was. There was only Jhurat.

"She has been traveling, as she said," Nasser continued after a moment, diplomatically opting not to comment on either fairy stories or mice, which was only one of the reasons he'd been Khaled's right hand and best friend since they'd been boys. "She flew to Scotland six months ago and has been wandering since, following what appears to be a largely whimsical itinerary south and east. One of those gap-year journeys, it seems, though she finished her university studies some years back. Perhaps she is 'finding herself'?"

Khaled snorted at his aide's dry tone. "And instead she found me. Poor little mouse."

"There is no need for you to deal with this situation any further if you don't wish it," the other man said then. "We can handle a girl. Especially one who cannot possibly cause a single ripple, no matter what becomes of her."

"And can you handle our enemies, too? Who even now work to have me removed from the palace because of my tainted blood?" What they whispered was that Khaled's line was weak, that the son would inherit his father's dementia before his time. And who was to say they were wrong? He shoved that aside. "I am certain they have already leaked the fact that I have a young female American in custody to the papers. It is inevitable."

"The papers can be dealt with."

"Our papers, perhaps." But that was how his father had done things, and look what it had wrought: this mess Khaled had to clean up, though he often doubted he could. He doubted anyone could, but it was his duty—his fate—to try anyway, no matter what happened. "But what happens when they take it to the international stage? Which they are certain to do." Because it was what he would do, and Khaled had the peculiar pleasure of knowing his enemies well. "How will we look to the world when I am painted as some kind of monster who abducts fresh-faced young American girls from the streets?"

He already knew what it would do to the contracts they needed to lock down to bring commerce to the country. To say nothing of the much-needed influx of international wealth, which, with the increase in tourism since he'd opened the borders again, might tip the scales in Khaled's favor. In Jhurat's favor, at long last.

He couldn't afford any backsliding. Not now.

"The people do not want to revert to the Stone Age," Nasser said darkly. "They want their movies and their technology right along with their paychecks from all the new jobs. No matter what that fool may tell himself."

"That fool" was Talaat, the leader of the resistance movement that opposed Khaled's claim to the sultanate with the assertion that Khaled's blood was tainted with the same infirmity of mind that had taken his father down.

Can we risk the country? Talaat liked to ask on the news and all over the papers, so reasonably.

Talaat was also Khaled's cousin on his mother's side. They'd played together as small boys. It made a kind of poetic sense that his own cousin should have become the greatest thorn in his side, Khaled thought, since he couldn't remember a single instance in which *his blood* had done anything but make his life harder, including Amira's stunt today.

"Talaat does not care what the people want," Khaled said shortly. "He cares about power."

Nasser didn't respond, because this was an unfortunate truth that might not matter in the least should Talaat's seditious behavior gain footholds in the proper places, and Khaled's mouth twisted in a wry sort of smile. It wouldn't do to become the next internet sensation at a time like this. It would take very little to tip public sentiment against him, and Americans, with their Kickstarter campaigns and their internet apps that could make civil unrest in faroff places into one more video game they could play from their couches, loved nothing more than to cry out against countries like Jhurat at the slightest provocation.

Or no provocation at all.

But that meant he had to think very carefully about what to do about the photogenic American girl who should never have crossed paths with Amira. What stories would she tell if he set her free? Who would listen to her when she told them? How would his enemies spin this story if they got their hands on her—and they would. He knew they would. They always did.

Inside the parlor, the girl shifted in her seat, then sat up, and Khaled studied her, bracing himself for what he knew he had to do. Had known since he'd pulled her out of that car, and if he was honest, was more interested in doing now that she'd shown him that surprising—if misguided—strength of hers.

She was a gift. And he would take all the gifts he could get.

As gifts went, he had to admit, she was an excellent one. She was delicate, with her large eyes and remarkably fine features, her hair a collection of reds, browns and caramels twisted inexpertly and pinned to the back of her head.

Pretty, something inside him noted, in a way that made him shift on his feet, then frown. *Too pretty.*

Elegant and unforgettable, in fact, with that face of hers and the coltish lines of her figure—yet she was dressed like a tomboy. Her clothes were deliberately mannish and casual in that Western style he'd never really understood during his studies abroad in England and the States, and which he most certainly did not appreciate in a woman.

Khaled was a traditional man. He had always preferred women who understood their own uniquely feminine appeal. Who boasted womanly hips and generous breasts to cushion a man in softness, instead of a boyish figure and too many bones besides. Women who offered him shy gazes to make him feel strong and musical voices to soothe him when he felt anything but. Demure and modest women, traditional women.

Not Western girls like this one in her androgynous clothes, flat-chested and skinny-thighed, who had stared back at him directly in the street, dared to scowl at him, and hadn't had the sense to beg for his mercy.

He couldn't remember the last time he'd found defiance anything but irritating.

And yet her eyes were extraordinary. More than extraordinary. They'd been filled with the setting sun out in that tiny little alleyway, and yet even when they weren't they were a kind of bright, gleaming gold, like ancient treasure, and he didn't understand why he couldn't get them out of his head.

Why it felt as if she haunted him, as if she had already worked her odd, scowling way into the heart of him when he should hardly have noticed her at all beyond her potential value to him. To his country.

Khaled told himself it was nothing more than strategy that made him walk inside that room then, whether he wanted to do it or not. Politics and power and the fate of his country besides.

Because it couldn't be anything else. He knew better.

"I apologize," he said, summoning up that charm of his that felt rusty from disuse, as though his smile was made from cut glass.

"And as it happens, I do require an apology," she said drily. "I accept."

But she stopped when her eyes met his, as if the sound of her own voice in the elegant room was alarming, somehow. Or he was.

"That regrettable scene in the street must have alarmed you, Miss Churchill."

She stared up at him in that same bright, golden way she had before, direct and clever at once, and Khaled couldn't name the thing that moved in him then, powerful and dark.

But he could use it. And he would. He would do anything for his country. Even this. *Especially this,* a rebellious little voice murmured deep inside him. *Maybe she is* your *gift.*

Khaled smiled wider and settled himself in the chair at an angle to the settee where she sat, looking delicate and amusingly put out against the bright cushions scattered around her—

Looking like the small, frightened mouse she is, he corrected himself. Caught between much larger and sharper claws than she could imagine. He leaned in closer, aware of the way her eyes widened slightly, the way her breath caught, and he knew it wasn't fear.

She was aware of him as a man. *Good*.

He'd use that, too.

Something unexpectedly hot wound through him when she licked her lips, her eyes still fixed on him. And then she frowned at him, and he liked it. Far more than he should.

"I hope you'll allow an overprotective brother to make it up to you as best he can," Khaled said, his smile even brighter.

He was going to enjoy this.

CHAPTER TWO

THE MAN WHO walked into that parlor as if it, too, should cower before him as he moved was fearful and breathtaking, but he wasn't quite the same one who had confronted Cleo in the street—and not only because he'd changed his clothes, she thought.

This version of the Sultan of Jhurat smiled as he sat down with her, something that altered that fierce face of his and made him nothing short of stunning.

Her heart pounded hard, like a fist against her ribs.

"Please," he said in a pleasant tone of voice, lounging there in a sleek buttoned black shirt over a pair of loose black trousers, neither of which made him look any less dangerous than he had in that alley. It was as if he'd traded in a scimitar for a polished knife, but the sharp edge was still the same. She'd never in her life met anyone so *male.* "You must call me Khaled."

As if they were friends. As if it was possible that one could *be* friends with a man like this. Cleo doubted it. He was far too intense, far too...*colossal.*

"Uh, okay. Khaled."

He looked as if he could eat a thousand Brians for breakfast and still be hungry.

She looked at the room instead of at him, hoping that might ease the clench of that bright heat inside her. But it didn't, no matter how many lovely silk pillows decorated the delicately pretty couches, or how much gold was on the ceiling and dripping down the walls into the exuberant sconces. No matter that *smile* on the sultan's darkly ferocious face as he looked at her now.

"Does this mean you're not planning to arrest me any longer?" she asked. Politely. And only then realized she was frowning.

He threw his head back and laughed. It was heart-stopping. Cleo felt as if she'd fallen down hard and knocked the breath straight out of her lungs.

"I'll confess to overreacting," he said, that astonishing laughter still rich in his dark voice. "It is an older brother's prerogative, surely."

He nodded at some unseen servant—and this was the sort of over-the-top place, preening with dramatic chandeliers draped in crystals and entire gleaming ballrooms lined with complicated tapestries depicting epic historical events she couldn't identify, that must have whole battalions of unseen servants, Cleo imagined—and sure enough, a tray appeared before them. Hot, fragrant tea and an array of treats, sweet and savory alike, as if he was trying to tempt her.

Or charm her.

And then the Sultan of Jhurat waved his servants away and poured tea for her, as if nothing in the world could be more normal than to serve her himself.

Her. Cleo Churchill from outside Columbus, Ohio, to whom absolutely nothing interesting had ever happened. Embarrassing and humiliating, sure. But a cheating fiancé wasn't *interesting*. It was boring, run-of-the-mill, exactly as she'd concluded she must have been if a safe and supposedly *good* man like Brian had been driven to betray her so completely.

She was dreaming, clearly. She'd thought so repeatedly over the past few hours, and her thigh ached from all the times she'd pinched it. She thought she'd have a bruise by morning, and still she found herself lost in the way he moved, all of that leashed strength and easy power obvious even in his handling of a delicate china teacup.

Cleo swallowed, hard, as though that might clear the buzzing in her ears. Or wake her up.

"Tea?" he asked smoothly, as if it were the most natural thing imaginable for a man like him to wait on her, in any capacity, when she could see it wasn't.

She could *see* the way he wore his command, so matter-of-factly. That it was a part of him. That the fierceness, the dark ruthlessness she'd seen in him before, was the truth of him. Not this creature, whoever he was, who smiled at her and made her blood heat.

Almost as if he *meant* to charm her... But that was absurd. She was far too practical to yearn for something so out of her reach. Wasn't she?

She ignored that insane voice inside her that whispered that after suffering through Brian, she *deserved* something this impossible. This wild and beautiful.

"I don't want to keep you," she said, but she took the cup and saucer he offered her anyway, as if her hands wanted things she wouldn't let herself wish for. Maybe that was why her voice came out so crisp when she spoke again, as though she was chastising him. "I'm sure you have any number of official duties to perform."

"None so pressing I can't take the time to correct a grave error," he said, settling back against his seat and training that intense gaze of his on her, gleaming with what she didn't think she dared call amusement. "I apologize for my sister, Miss Churchill. She dragged you into a family matter and put you in a terrible position. It's unforgivable."

"Cleo. If I'm to call you Khaled—" and there was something about his name that felt different against her tongue then, like a square of dark, almost-bitter chocolate, and a light flared briefly in his slate-gray gaze as though he tasted it, too "—you should certainly call me Cleo."

"Is that short for Cleopatra?" he asked almost lazily, making her wish it was. Making her wish with a sudden deep fervor that she could transform herself into whatever might please him—and she didn't know where that thought came from. Only that she felt it like her own too-warm blood, pounding through her, changing her where she sat.

But then, she'd been there, done that, with a man who could never dream of being Khaled's equal. She wouldn't do it again.

"No." She set down the tea without tasting it, afraid she'd drop the whole of it on the undoubtedly priceless rug beneath her dusty feet. "My mother liked it."

He studied her for a moment, until she realized she was holding her breath.

"I like it, too," he said, and she didn't understand the heat that blasted through her, confusing her even as it made her ache.

"You were talking about your sister," she reminded him, somehow ignoring that thing that wound ever tighter deep inside her.

"Amira is my responsibility," he said after a moment, that hard voice of his a shade warmer, though not at all soft. "Our mother died when she was quite small and I suppose I feel as much a parent to her as an older brother. And I regret I've not been there for her as I should have. My father's health has declined quite seriously in the past year and my attention has been on the country. That is not an excuse and not something I could have changed, but it is a factor, I think, in her acting out."

"I don't know that it's possible to really be there for a teenage girl," she said after a moment, when she was reasonably certain her voice would come out even. "No matter who she is. Feeling abandoned and mistreated is par for the course, as I remember it, whether that's true or not."

"I can't help thinking that she would do better with a female's guidance. Someone to look up to who is not the autocratic brother who now makes all the decisions about her life that she doesn't much like. I suspect she finds me as baffling as I find her."

It took Cleo a moment to look up, because she'd been too busy staring at the frayed cuffs of the dark trousers she'd worn in too many countries to count and wondering with only the faintest little hint of despair why she was dressed like a teenage girl when she wasn't one. Sitting here in this place—in this *palace*—she'd never been more aware of how far short she fell of any kind of womanly ideal.

She was a little bit of a mess, if she was honest. Ragged cuffs, torn-off fingernails, worn and battered clothes that she'd been wearing for six months straight and washing out in a hundred hostel sinks. Backpacker chic didn't translate in a *palace,* she understood, especially when she was sitting in the presence of a man who made even what she assumed were his casual clothes look impossibly splendid.

You let yourself go, Cleo, Brian had said, as if that were a reasonable explanation for lying and cheating. *And we're not even married yet. I wanted someone who would never do that.*

And I wanted someone who wouldn't sleep with other people, Brian, *so I guess my ratty jeans are my business,* she'd snapped back at him.

And then what Khaled had said penetrated and she lifted her gaze to find him watching her much too intently, a thousand things she didn't understand in those slate-gray eyes of his. It made her shiver. It made her wonder.

It made her understand her own insecurities.

Brian was a spoiled child but Khaled was very plainly

a man—and a man used to the best of everything, surrounded by beauty on every side. Even his tea set shouted out its delicate, resolute prettiness. Was it insane that she wished she was as pretty, as lovely, as all these things he was used to having around him?

That he might look at *her* and find her beautiful, too?

Of course it's insane, she scolded herself. *If Brian thought you dressed as though you let yourself go, what must* the Sultan of Jhurat *think?*

"The best cure for teenage girls is the passage of time," Cleo said, curling her lamentable fingernails into her palms and out of sight. Time was also the best cure for embarrassment, she'd found, though there were new humiliations all the time, apparently. "I speak as someone who used to be one. The only way out is through, I promise you."

She had Brian in her head again, and she hated it. He didn't deserve to take up any space inside her. How had she ever believed otherwise?

"And is this why you have traveled so long and so far?" Khaled asked after a moment. "To give yourself this time?"

"I haven't been a teenage girl in quite a while." It was almost as if she wanted to make sure he knew she was a grown woman, and Cleo refused to analyze why on earth she should want that. She shifted in her seat, trying to ease that clenched, knotted thing inside her. "This was more to prove that I could."

"Why was that something that required proof?" asked a man who, she imagined, wouldn't have to prove himself. Ever.

No one would cheat on this man. No one would dare.

"I had a decent job in a nice office doing human resources. Family and friends and a perfectly good routine. I was doing everything I was supposed to do," she said, and it sounded mechanical. Or tasted that way in her mouth. She shrugged. "But in the end, I wanted more."

"More?" he asked.

More than what waited for her in the wake of a broken engagement in a town full of pity and averted gazes. More than the weak man she had nearly tied herself to, so stupidly. More than *Brian*.

"It sounds silly," she said.

There was no way that she could tell him the real reason she'd walked out of Brian's condo and straight into a travel agency the next morning. There was no way she could admit how blind and foolish she'd been. Not to this man, who was looking at her as though she was neither of those things.

She never wanted to look at a man like this and see *pity*. She thought it might kill her.

Khaled smiled, and there was nothing like pity on his hard face. "I cannot tell if it does or does not, if you do not say it."

"My entire life was laid out in front of me." Brian hadn't wanted to break up, after all. That had been all Cleo's doing. And Brian hadn't been the only one who'd thought her reaction to what he'd deemed his "minor indiscretion" was more than a little overdramatic. *Life isn't a fairy tale,* her sister Marnie had said with a sniff. *You might as well learn that now.* Cleo forced a smile. "It's a very nice life. I could probably have been content with it. Lots of people are. And I have deep roots in the place I came from, which means something."

"Yet you were not happy." He studied her for a moment, and she had to fight the urge to look away from that level stare lest he see all the things she didn't want him to know. "You perhaps wanted wings instead of roots."

It was such a simple flash of light, like joy, to be understood so matter-of-factly by a man like this, who was himself so far beyond her experience. But Cleo didn't know what to do with it, so she pushed on.

"I decided I needed to do something big." She'd wanted to disappear, in fact, and this was the next best thing. She lifted her hands, then remembered that she was hiding them and dropped them back in her lap. "And it's a big world."

"So we are told."

Cleo almost thought he was laughing. She didn't want to examine how very much she wished he was.

"I wanted more," she said again, and there was that fierce note in her voice that she knew was as much bitterness as it was the bone-deep stubbornness that had had her on a plane out of Ohio barely forty-eight hours after walking in on Brian and his girlfriend. "Unfortunately, when you say something like that, the people who *are* content think that you're saying their lives are small in comparison."

"Most lives *are* small," he said, this *sultan,* and Cleo forgot herself.

She laughed. "How would you know?"

Their eyes caught then, his gaze startled, and she didn't know which one of them was more surprised.

But she refused to let herself apologize, the way some part of her wanted to do.

"You can laugh at yourself, you know," she said without meaning to open her mouth again. "It won't kill you."

His dark gray eyes gleamed. Something Cleo couldn't quite identify moved over his face, making her pulse and shiver low in her belly. "Are you quite certain?"

And somehow, she was wordless.

"In any event," he said after a moment, still in that dry, amused tone she could scarcely believe, "you are not wrong. My life has been many things, but not, as you say, small."

He waved a negligent hand, *sultanlike* if she'd had to define it, beckoning her to continue. And Cleo did, because at this point, what was there to lose? She had already taken that dive. Might as well swim.

"When I bought my plane tickets, things got a bit tense." That was as true as the rest, if not quite the full story. But she wasn't going to tell this man about the accusations she'd fielded. That she was harsh and cold and *unrealistic,* that she was frigid besides, that *she* was the problem— because six months later she still didn't know if any of it was true. And what if Khaled agreed with Brian's assessment of her? She found she was scowling at him again, but she didn't care. "But I don't believe that anyone should have to settle for someone. Or something. Or *anything.* I think that's what people tell themselves to make themselves feel better about choices they can't take back. And I don't want to settle. I won't."

Khaled was definitely smiling then, an indulgent curve to those warrior's lips, and it made her stomach flip over. Then again. As if she'd been spouting poetry instead of ranting a bit too intensely.

"You are not an ordinary girl," he said, and Cleo should have found that patronizing. She should have been insulted. Instead she felt molten and consumed, somehow, by that intent gleam in his dark gaze. Or the fact that she thought she'd do anything to keep him looking at her like that. As if he thought she might be marvelous. "In fact, I think you are quite a fascinating woman, aren't you, Cleo?"

And she wanted him to think so. She wanted that more than she wanted to admit, even to herself. She could have sworn he knew that, too. That it was obvious to him, and reflected in that crook of his hard mouth.

"You're very kind," she said.

"You told me before that you have only two weeks left in this trip of yours." She was stunned that he remembered anything about her and found herself nodding, her eyes fixed on him, burned and breathless at once. "I have a suggestion, Cleo, and I hope you'll consider it."

"Of course." She told herself her voice wasn't gauzy, insubstantial. That she was simply speaking softly for a change.

"Stay here for your last two weeks," he urged her.

He leaned forward then and her heart nearly somersaulted from her chest when he reached over and took her hand in his, enveloping her in a wallop of heat. All of that heat and strength and power from his simple touch like a drug inside her, making her heavy and giddy. Dizzy and drunk.

Captured more surely than if he'd locked her up in a cell after all.

His gaze met hers, and she might have been crazy but she could have sworn that all the things she was feeling, all that wildness and fire, he felt, too.

For a moment, there was nothing at all but the two of them.

"Stay with me," he said softly, and it didn't occur to her to do anything at all but agree.

Cleo's battered blue backpack waited for her in the rooms she'd been told were hers for the rest of her stay, a little touch of reality in the midst of what felt like fantasy on top of fantasy. Because what Khaled had casually referred to as her *rooms* were in fact part of a luxurious, palatial bedroom suite straight out of those fairy tales her sister sniffed at.

Rich reds decked the high walls, the vast, deep bed was piled deep with pillows in various jewel shades, and the whole of it was shaded by a gloriously sheer canopy that floated above like a dream. Sumptuous rugs were thrown across every inch of the floor in riots of complicated patterns and colors that should have clashed or felt loud and garish, yet didn't. Intricate lattice-worked shutters in dark woods graced the many windows and led out to a long balcony, stunning works of art hung on the walls, and complex mosaics were inlaid in the high ceilings and arches. All of that and a sitting room, a dressing room and a closet that rivaled the size of most apartments back home, and a gloriously decadent bath that Cleo could have swum laps in, had she wanted.

There was even a smiling, deferential maid named Karima who fluttered around Cleo as if she were some kind of princess, urging her into the bath that first night and then into a dress she'd never seen before when she got out.

"This isn't mine," Cleo protested, her fingers rough against the astonishing smoothness of the deep blue material, the prettiest thing she thought she'd ever felt, slippery and fine against her woefully neglected hands. "I can't…"

"The sultan insists," Karima replied, as if that ended the conversation.

As if that *was* the conversation.

If she was staying here, Cleo had decided during her long, luxurious soak, then she would have to make certain that Khaled realized it was her choice to do so, not his command.

But when she was led into the small private dining room later that evening, Cleo felt as if she'd been transformed into a dream version of herself, and it was hard to remember why there was something wrong about that.

The dress the sultan insisted she wear was long and more elegant than anything she'd ever worn in her life, bare about the shoulders and then swishing over her legs as she walked to make her feel almost shivery, while her feet felt naked in the sandals she'd been given. Her hair had been brushed out and left to swirl around her shoulders in a shining mass that flowed when she moved, and

Karima had even slicked a gloss over her lips. It was all overwhelmingly sensual, somehow.

The sultan waited for her in the small dining room arranged around a gurgling fountain with windows that opened over a lush and fragrant interior courtyard, as if they weren't in a desert at all. He was still dressed all in black, with a jacket over the shirt he'd worn earlier, which made him look as elegant as a hard man could.

And when he turned to greet her, Cleo froze. One of the benefits of never having tried to be the kind of sleek, elegant woman Brian had wanted was that she'd always imagined that *if she'd wanted to,* she could have transformed herself.

But this was as transformed as she'd ever be, and she knew it. And she felt more naked before this man than she ever had without her clothes.

His dark, cool gaze moved over her, taking in everything from the spill of blue fabric to the silver of the sandals she wore. This was torment, she thought. This was beyond embarrassing—

His gaze lifted to hers at last, and Cleo's breath left her in a rush at the approval she saw gleaming there. The heat that roared in her in response. Relief and pleasure mixed into one, because if he believed in this version of her she thought she could, too.

Khaled wasn't Brian. The notion was laughable. Khaled looked at her as though she was as beautiful as he was, not as if he were doing her a favor. How could she find that anything but intoxicating?

"Thank you for indulging me," he said, as if he could see her uncertainty. As if he knew all that odd terror and tumult, pleasure and need, inside her. "I fear I am more traditional than is fashionable these days, but I find nothing so beautiful as a pretty woman in a lovely dress."

Cleo smiled. How could she do anything but smile?

And when he held out his hand, a certain satisfaction in his cool gaze that she knew should probably have worried her, she ignored that little prickle of doubt—and took it.

"You can't keep giving me things," Cleo told him very seriously a few mornings into her stay, with another fierce and wholly inappropriate frown he found uncomfortably adorable.

Khaled had taken to having long, leisurely breakfasts with her, an indulgence he had no time for but allowed anyway. He liked to lounge there in the small nook he never normally used, strewn with pillows and streaming with sunlight, and watch her as she chased the sleep from those golden-hued eyes of hers with each sip of the strong coffee she liked.

Every day, he was more familiar with her. He touched her hand, her arm, her leg. He was intrigued by every caught breath, every shiver, that she worked so hard to hide from him. Today he reached over and tugged gently at the end of the ponytail she wore, until her honey gaze swung to his, all of that awareness simmering there, the way he wanted it.

He wanted a great deal more than he'd expected he would. He told himself that was no more than the lure of the chase, the excitement of this game. But that low, hard heat he couldn't seem to dispel whispered otherwise.

"I prefer your hair down," he said, his voice a low rumble, and he liked the flush that warmed her skin at the sound. Why was it so hard to maintain his control around this woman? He knew what the boundaries were. He knew he had to tempt her to fall, not push her over the edge. He knew what he was doing. "I like to see the light in it."

"Khaled." She had to struggle to keep her voice even, he could hear. It was more of a struggle every day, and he liked that, too. Her hands moved to her hair, then dropped to her lap. "You can't."

"This is Jhurat, is it not?" He was teasing her, and he liked the way she melted into it, as though she wanted to resist him, yet couldn't.

"You know perfectly well it is."

"And am I not the Sultan of Jhurat?"

"That's the rumor," she said drily, making him laugh. He hadn't expected that she'd amuse him—and, he reminded himself, it didn't matter if she did. It was beside the point.

Though it makes this that much sweeter, a traitorous little voice whispered, as if he was like other men. As if he had choices.

As if she did.

"Then I believe I can do as I like." He shrugged. "It pleases me to give you things, Cleo." This time when he reached out to her, he traced a gentle pattern from her temple to her cheek, something hot moving in him when she trembled. "Don't you want to please me?" He didn't wait for her answer, even though he knew what she'd say. It was too soon. "Be careful how you answer that. There are laws."

She laughed, as he'd intended, and he liked that, too.

The American was his. As planned.

"You realize you will break her heart," Nasser said one evening after being forced to interrupt one of the increasingly intimate dinners Khaled had insisted Cleo share with him.

Khaled shot him a cool look as they walked through the palace's wide, ornate halls toward an impromptu meeting of his security council to focus on yet another one of Talaat's attempts to stir up trouble in the provinces.

"I will note your concern for her," he said as they went,

his voice more clipped than it should have been. As if he cared, when he knew he couldn't. "In the meantime you can comfort yourself with the knowledge that I know precisely how far I need to push her. And where I must stop."

"I only wonder if it is necessary to go quite so far," Nasser said in that same calm way of his. "Perhaps there is a kinder way to achieve your ends."

"There is no power on this earth more motivating than falling in love," Khaled said grimly, and told himself that he felt nothing. "It can make the most practical among us do precisely what we know we shouldn't. And then, soon enough, it disappears when reality sets in. That is the time for kindness."

You feel nothing, he barked at himself. No twist of regret, no sorrow for what might have been. No yearning for all the ways he could have lost himself in the glory of her instant, artless response to him, were he a different man.

Because the moment Cleo had let Amira into her car, she'd thrust herself into the middle of a chess game Khaled had no choice but to play—and play to win. And he would.

"The only greater power is that of love scorned," was his friend's reply. "As I think you know all too well."

"Cleo is not my mother." Khaled rubbed his hands over his face, annoyed that this was even a topic of conversation when the country hung in the balance, when he was only doing what he must in the most expedient manner possible. "My little mouse is not going to rise up one day and surprise us with her claws, then expedite her own destruction. That's not who she is."

Nasser inclined his head and moved to open the door to the briefing room.

"And more importantly, I am not my father," Khaled found himself saying, dark and furious. Unbearably defensive. "I know what I'm doing."

"As you say, Your Excellency," Nasser murmured deferentially.

Which was, Khaled knew, no response at all.

But he had no choice.

And even if he'd had a choice, he knew he'd do this the exact same way. That was the thing that stuck in him, making Nasser's words echo too loudly inside him, making him feel hollow. Because he was a selfish man, when all was said and done. Exactly as his father had been. When he was alone, when no one could see him or try to read the expressions on his face, he accepted that.

But it didn't change a thing.

At least his father hadn't *meant* to do what he'd done. Khaled would have no such excuse. He would protect Cleo from the worst of it, from his own mother's fate—but he couldn't bring himself to save her from himself.

Khaled knew what that made him. A monster of his own design.

Some nights later they strolled together through the moonlit courtyard. Cleo looked like quicksilver in the moonlight, very nearly ethereal, and when she smiled at him over her shoulder as she argued with him about some foolish book he'd told her was pointless, it clutched at him.

He'd made her inarguably beautiful with only a different wardrobe and two weeks. It was high time he made her *his,* no matter what kind of monster that made him.

She hadn't put her hair up since the day he'd told her he liked it down. She'd stopped fighting the clothes he gave her, the trinkets he left for her to wear. And he found that the more he watched her and the more she bloomed from an awkward, androgynous Westerner into a woman possessed of the studied elegance he preferred, this delicate creature who frowned at him and talked back to him, the more he thought she was the perfect choice. The world would consider her a great beauty, he knew, with her natural slenderness and innate grace, and it would make them sigh over this romance he was shaping in precisely the way he wanted.

And he would always remember this. Here. Now. When she was half in love with him already. When she was lost in him and greedy for his touch. When she didn't have the slightest idea what their future would look like.

It surprised him how very deep and powerful that pleasure ran, so atavistic, so rudimentary, it was almost indistinguishable from need. From the kind of hunger that he couldn't indulge—the kind that would wreck not only the both of them, but all his carefully crafted plans besides.

He needed her to teeter on the edge, he reminded himself sternly. Not to fall.

"You aren't listening to me," she said then, rolling her eyes in a deeply disrespectful manner that should have offended him, yet didn't. "That's considered rude in both our cultures, I think you'll find."

You will break her heart, Nasser had warned him. But then, Khaled had never claimed to be a good man. Only a determined one.

And, oh, such a selfish one.

"Have you become so brave, then?" he asked into the silvery moonlight, lazy and flirtatious, ignoring the darkness beneath that he didn't care to acknowledge. "That you would dare to scold a sultan?"

He reached over and took her hands in his, and that heat in him deepened, caught fire. He hadn't expected to want her, particularly not with that jagged edge too much like raw need, but Khaled told himself that he could control it.

Because he had to control it. Because he *was not* his father.

"I dare," she said, but her voice was little more than a shimmer in the dark, and he smiled.

"Come here," he said, and tugged her to him.

She came easily, as he'd expected. Her breath came short and hard, as though she was running flat-out, and the moon made her eyes gleam, wide and filled with longing—and it wasn't in him to resist her.

He didn't try.

"Kiss me," he said, a silken order against the night. "If you are so daring."

He could feel her tremble against him, and he liked it. She tilted her head back, and he liked the fire in her golden gaze, and the hunger that very nearly matched his. He wanted to taste her, suddenly, as if he'd never wanted anything else.

As if he wasn't as in control as he wanted to believe he was.

Cleo shifted up onto her toes, bracing herself against his chest, and he liked that too much to worry about control. She was feminine, elegant and sweet in the dresses she wore for him, her hair a tempting fall all around her simply because he liked it. She smelled like jasmine, sweet and soft and his. *His.*

First he would taste her. Then he'd control this—her—the way he knew he should have done all along.

Cleo shifted closer. He held her there, waiting, drawing it out, until he didn't know which one of them was more needy. *Just one taste,* he told himself.

He let her lean into him, against him, pressing into his chest. And that dark, stalking thing inside him roared, predatory and hungry—

And then Cleo went up on her toes, put her sweet mouth to his, and everything simply exploded.

CHAPTER THREE

DESIRE ROCKETED THROUGH Khaled like a searing comet, sudden and fierce and stunning. It was an ambush. It burned him alive, nearly taking him out at the knees, nearly dropping him to the stones below.

He'd never felt anything like this. It was a bone-deep, all-encompassing madness. It changed everything. It made his heart slam against his chest, made his blood a sweet, unbearable fire in his veins, made him hard and desperate, greedy for *more*.

More of her lips, her scent, her softness. The wonder of her slender body pressed against him like a live wire. More of that humming awareness that tipped over into pounding, dizzying need. More of the shocked, excited noises she made in her throat, the lushness of her lips, the slick drag of her mouth over his.

Her kiss was a revelation and a curse, and he stopped thinking, stopped plotting. He forgot who he was, why he was doing this. He stopped playing his games, stopped teasing her, stopped worrying about strategy.

He felt primitive. Alive. *Desperate.* One hand rose to tangle in her hair, holding her head where he wanted it. The other slid to her hip and pulled her close, tighter.

And then he simply took her.

He feasted on her mouth, losing himself in the slide of her tongue against his, the perfection of that mouth of hers he hadn't understood was so tempting, so blatantly erotic. She tasted like honey and made him long to taste her everywhere.

Made him long to simply lift her against him, part her delicate thighs and take her where they stood. The need in his blood was like a song, a velvet command.

The kiss was carnal and hot. Khaled felt like a glutton and a god, and she was his. *His.* Yielding to him and testing him, tasting him and arousing him in turn, and he couldn't seem to get enough.

Never enough, something hissed inside him, dazed and deliriously intrigued. *Never enough of this. Of her.*

This was no lazy dance toward sensuality, as he'd intended. This was a great deal more than a *taste.* This was fire. Need. A dark, disastrous blaze of hunger that Khaled couldn't control, and while he lost himself in the exquisite feel of her, the addictive taste, he didn't care the way he knew he should.

The way some part of him imagined he would—but he shoved that aside.

He didn't know when they moved, when he did, but he took her with him as he sat on one of the stone benches. He pulled her across his lap, her knees on either side of him, the soft heat of her pressed tight against the hardest part of him.

Cleo sighed, and the yearning in the sound only made him hungrier. Moonlight bathed her in silver, making shadows of her lovely eyes, but not hiding that heat. That need. The starkness of the shocking desire that he could no more deny in either of them than he could rise up and fly away.

He tugged her mouth back to his and it was the same hot punch. The same wildfire, pulling tight inside him, demanding he take her. Right now. Right here. Again and again, until the spell she cast was broken. Or until she cried out his name and her need in that voice of hers gone husky with passion. Or until this madness killed them both, and he didn't think he'd mind the dying.

He used his mouth to follow the line of her jaw, then tasted the delicate skin she bared when she tipped her head back, allowing him access. He tasted her collarbone, then moved lower, until he reached the bodice of her dress.

Khaled didn't hesitate. He'd always preferred larger breasts on his women and yet when he peeled the fabric away, the sight of hers, small and plump at once, delicate curves and taut nipples, almost undid him.

"Khaled," she whispered, a broken sound, honeyed and rough, like gas thrown on open flame.

He slid his hand over her left breast, abrading the tight peak with his palm, watching her expressive face as her eyes drifted shut and she pulled her bottom lip between her teeth.

She was a wonder. She was *his*. He increased the pressure and her hips bucked against him, a rocking, rolling ecstasy that shot fire into every part of him and made her breath catch audibly. A rosy sort of flush stole over her, almost as if...

He couldn't resist.

Khaled bent his head to her other breast and licked over her nipple, then pulled the proud crest into his mouth. Hard.

And Cleo broke apart in his arms, shuddering and sighing, flushed red and wild, and he understood that he was in deep trouble with this woman, after all.

When Cleo came back to herself, she felt weak and boneless—and ashamed, slumped as she was in Khaled's arms. He'd shifted her, holding her in his arms rather than astride him, and she could sense the difference and the distance in him at once.

What must he think of her? That she was a wanton

slut, to start. That she was so oversexed she came apart at a *lick* against the completely wrong part of her body. She shuddered, appalled at herself—and mourning this glorious dream he'd allowed her to live over the past two weeks that she'd no doubt tarnished with her horrendous lack of restraint.

And then, as swiftly, she was furious. Almost blindingly so.

"I'm sorry," she bit out into the night, because she didn't dare look at his face. "Is there a 'no touching the sultan' rule I didn't know about? You should have said so."

"Do not ever apologize for your responsiveness," he said, his voice cool but dry, too, as if he was amused by her outburst. "Or for falling apart in my arms. These are gifts."

Cleo struggled to sit up and he let her, but embarrassment pumped through her as she pulled away from him, making her feel obvious and strange. She could still feel the magic of his touch spinning around inside her, making her skin too tight and her head fuzzy, but she concentrated on straightening her dress as if, once she was appropriately covered, it would erase the whole thing. Make everything right and wonderful again.

Make her something other than humiliated.

But her body had other ideas. Her nipples were like white-hot lights, blasting her with leftover sensation, and between her legs, she ached. She *ached*.

"I didn't mean for that to happen," she said. Stiff and cold.

He shifted on the stone bench beside her and the moon high above them made him gleam like poured metal, as though he was a statue of himself. All of that power, that corded strength, and she'd finally felt it beneath her hands. Her palms itched with the memory, the imprint. She thought of his demanding mouth on hers and something within her melted and then ran hot.

"How many lovers have you had?" he asked, and she jolted as if he'd doused her with ice water.

"What?" But she thought only of Brian, who she'd rather die than claim as a lover. Especially now.

"How many?"

"I don't want to answer that," she said, slowly but distinctly. "Or think it's any of your business. Why would you ask?"

Khaled only looked at her, for such a long time that she began to feel too aware of the cool air against her still-flushed skin again. So long that she crossed her arms over her chest and told herself the cold she felt came from the temperature of the night air, not from him.

And then, as her temper ebbed, she found herself answering him anyway.

"There's no answer I can give to that question that will make this moment anything but awkward. More awkward, I mean," she said, and his lips twitched, the way they did when she made him laugh.

"Luckily, awkwardness has yet to claim a single death, as far as I know."

"How many lovers have *you* had?" she asked instead of answering him.

"I've had my share," he replied, that strange intensity in his cool gaze. "But I'm afraid I cannot accept that answer from you, Cleo."

"That sounds suspiciously like a nasty double standard," she said, striving for a light tone. And failing.

He shrugged in that way of his that reminded her how powerful he was. "It is. But I have never claimed to be particularly liberated and I still wish to know."

He said it as if knowing such personal details about her life were his right. And there was something about that air of authority, that tone of command in his cool voice, that made her long to do as he asked. Despite the huge part of her that didn't *want* to do it.

"One," Cleo said, grudgingly. "We met in college. We were supposed to get married." She scowled at him. "We didn't."

"When?"

Cleo told herself she only imagined that tightness in his voice, that stillness in the way he sat there, watching her. Waiting for her answer.

She didn't want to say another word. But it seemed that her mouth obeyed him all on its own.

"Six months ago."

His dark eyes were hooded then, impossible to read. He reached over and tucked her hair behind her ear, and she had to fight off the urge to lean into his touch.

"Ah," he said. "You wanted more than him."

She was furious again, and she wasn't sure why. "That, and I walked in on him with his girlfriend two weeks before our wedding."

His brows rose in surprise and she was so furious it was dizzying. And ashamed. And something about that particular toxic combination made her pulse clatter through her, jittery and wild.

"In case you're wondering why, don't." She wanted to get this over with, she realized suddenly. Make him pity her so she could stop pretending there was any other end to this magical interlude in her life. "He was quite clear that I'm frigid."

Khaled's expression shifted into something sad and dangerous at once, and he reached over and traced his fingertips down her cheek, slowly. She didn't know why she imagined it was some kind of apology. Then he took her chin in his hand, holding her immobile before him.

"You are many things," he said softly. Starkly. "But you are not, as we have demonstrated, even remotely frigid."

She should pull away, she knew. She should *do* something—but the air between them was so taut, so tense, and she couldn't read him. His gaze was too dark, his mouth too cruel, and she was dressed in clothes he'd given her, her body still trembling and tingling from his mouth, and the truth was that she didn't *want* to pull away from him.

Cleo wanted *him*. And yet Brian loomed between them, soft and deceitful and ruinous.

"They told me to marry him anyway," she told Khaled fiercely, as if it were a weapon. "That I was naive and silly to expect fidelity. That such romantic notions were unrealistic. The stuff of fantasy."

"Don't worry." It occurred to her that his tone of voice was lethal, but he was still holding her chin and the heat of that felt like a drug, making her feel heavy and weightless at once. Trapped with no desire whatsoever to set herself free. "I prize that particular fantasy above all others. And I am the ruler here. If I deem something realistic, that's what it is."

Her mind was a riot of *shoulds*, and she heeded none of them. There was something harsh in his face, his gaze, something too close to broken, when he'd said similar things in the past with a laugh.

"But do you mean your fidelity or mine?" she whispered. "They're not the same thing and some men, I've discovered, apply their double standards there more than anywhere else."

Khaled muttered something that sounded like a curse but which she imagined was a little prayer instead. He let her go.

She wished he was touching her again immediately. She was a lunatic. But she could feel the imprint of his fingers on her chin as if he'd stamped her with his heat. And she throbbed everywhere else.

"You will be the death of me, little mouse," he told

her, so low and quiet she thought for a minute she'd heard him wrong.

"I'm not a mouse." Something kicked in her. "The next time someone cheats on me, I'm drawing blood. Just so you know."

For a moment he looked almost proud, as if he approved of her bloodthirstiness, but then another shadow claimed his face, and she couldn't read him. Khaled stood then, and she felt as though the world was spinning all around him. He looked troubled, tortured. Like the stranger her heart no longer considered him.

"What's the matter?" she asked, her voice too rough. Too many emotions racking her within.

"Nothing at all," he said, and she knew, somehow, that he lied. "Come."

He offered her his arm and she rose to take it, incapable of defying him in that moment though there was that part of her that thought she should. That wanted her to *fight, damn it*—though she didn't know what for. He led her back into the palace, then down the polished, gleaming halls toward her suite, and it took him a long time to look at her again.

Cleo felt the lack of his attention like a kind of grief. Harsh and heavy.

"This is ridiculous," she said when they reached her door, her voice a prickle. A tight scratch against the heaviness between them. "You shouldn't have asked the question if you didn't want to hear the answer."

"The only answer I really needed was the way you came under my tongue," he said, but there was a distance in the way he said it. Something granite and unyielding beneath those words. "The rest was merely curiosity."

Cleo faced him then, her back to her door, and tried to read his dark, fierce face.

"Then you really shouldn't look so sad, should you?"

He laughed then, abruptly, and it wasn't the laughter she'd heard from him at other times that had warmed her deep within. This was hollow. Dark. This hurt both of them, she thought, and she didn't know why.

"Sadness is for men with choices," he told her, very distinctly, as if it was critical she understand this. Him. "I have only duty. It governs everything I do. It always has and it always will." His voice lowered. Roughened. "Remember that, Cleo. If nothing else."

"That sounds remarkably dire." And then, not knowing how she managed it, when he looked so grim and she simply hurt, she grinned at him. "It was only a kiss, Khaled. I think we'll survive."

He let out another one of those laughs that cut at her, even deeper this time.

"You don't know your own doom when it stares you in the face." He shook his head, and she didn't understand why he sounded so *agonized*. "How can I protect you when you won't protect yourself?"

Cleo didn't know what madness moved in her then, but she reached over and slid her hand against his lean jaw, as though that might comfort him. As though she could soothe him.

As though he was hers.

"It's going to be okay," she whispered, though she didn't even know what was wrong. "I promise."

Khaled froze, his gray eyes like a thunder that rolled in her, too, a warning she knew she should heed, but that same electricity leaped between them again, searing her straight through as though it was brand-new.

He muttered something beneath his breath, and then he leaned in close and took her mouth with all the passion and ruthless command he'd shown in the courtyard, and she was lost.

He tasted like the night and all the tumultuous stars

above. Like heat and dreams and that wildness inside her she'd never experienced before. Her hands moved against his chest, up into his thick, dark hair. He came even closer then, even more demanding, pulling her hands up to either side of her head and holding them there as he pressed her back against the door to her suite with the sweet, hot glory of his magnificent torso.

He was muttering in Arabic, low and intense, against her lips and then against her skin. It felt like licks of flame, enticing and delicious. Cleo curled her fingers around his, closed her eyes and fell off the edge of the world.

He was so hard against her, so big and beautiful, like a red-hot monolith. His shoulders were a wonder of lean, smooth muscle and then his hard thigh moved between her legs, until she was melting against him, her whole body shivering as if he could throw her straight over that cliff into bliss again. That easily.

She had no doubt he could, and it scared her—but she channeled it all into that delirious slide of lips and tongues, the rude and delicious rocking of his hard thigh directly against the aching heart of her need, the unmistakable sounds of his mastery and her own thrilling capitulation.

Nothing mattered but this. Nothing mattered but him.

The fire raged higher. Khaled simply stroked her, his tongue and his thigh in stunning, overwhelming concert, and she was already shuddering, so close, *so close*—

"Enough," he grated out, as if it hurt him.

He released her and stepped back, and she nearly sank to the ground, unable to process the tornado of sensation swirling in her, much less the fact that he'd stopped. He reached over and held her upright, that big hand of his wrapped tightly around one arm while his dark gaze burned into her.

Cleo could only stare at him, her breath coming too fast, her whole body in revolt, all that drugging, delicious passion still at a fever pitch inside her. She felt drugged. Altered and exposed, and the way he looked at her didn't help.

"I will not take you up against the wall like some common whore," he bit out, and it occurred to her to wonder if he wasn't swept away in the same storm of insane lust that she was, despite the hectic glitter in his gaze. He scowled at her. "I am the Sultan of Jhurat, not a drunken sailor on his first shore leave in years."

She didn't know which felt like more of a slap, but the red flush that swallowed her whole then wasn't passion any longer. It was shame. And then temper, like a vicious kick to her gut.

"You told me to kiss you out in the courtyard and just now *you* kissed *me*," she threw at him, embarrassed and frustrated and utterly lost in this, whatever it was. "You can't do that and then turn around and call *me* the whore unless you're willing to call yourself the same!"

He blinked as if no one had ever shouted at him before. Perhaps no one had. "I beg your pardon?"

"You're doing this, not me," she told him, confusion and temper swamping her. "Gowns and jewels and all the rest of this. What happened in the courtyard. What happened right now. Fidelity and sworn duty and I don't even know what this *is*."

Khaled's other hand moved, and he frowned as if he didn't have control over it as he dragged his thumb over her faintly swollen lips. His own mouth was a straight line, and his gaze had gone dark and brooding, the gray of long Februaries and winters without end, and still beautiful. Always so beautiful.

"I know what this is," he said, but if she'd thought he would expand on that, she was disappointed when he only shook his head as if to clear it and then looked away.

"I leave in three days." The spike of temper had drained away and now Cleo felt exhausted and too tired, with a dangerous prick of heat at the back of her eyes that warned her she might cry at any moment. She couldn't allow that. "I don't know what you want, Khaled."

A trace of that elusive humor on his hard face. "I think you do."

"Only not in the hall like a drunken sailor," she snapped, her chin rising with her temper. "And only after you decide whether or not I've slept with too many people."

He looked amazed at her temerity and entirely too forbidding, but she didn't care. Or back down.

"Put your claws away," he ordered her. "I didn't hurt you."

He was wrong about that, but she didn't want to enlighten him if he couldn't see it himself. If it wasn't obvious.

If there was any possibility at all that she could survive the rest of this with her dignity intact.

"Khaled." His name in her mouth seemed to surprise them both, urgent and rough. "There's no need to drag this out. You asked me to stay. If you want me to go, say so."

He shook his head then, his mouth in a grimmer line, his gaze dark and serious, and she didn't know why it made her ache like this. Why it hurt *so much* when he'd promised her nothing. He'd only treated her like that fantasy version of herself—the elegant, beautiful, beloved Cleo Churchill she'd never dared dream she could become, because she knew better.

Because Brian had taught her better, hadn't he?

"No, Cleo, I don't want you to go." Khaled shoved his hands in his pockets as if he was afraid they might do something against his will, and that made her breath catch again though there was a storm she could see right there on his face, raging on despite the smooth silk of his voice.

He shifted, yet never moved that gaze of his from hers, and she wanted that to matter. "I want you to marry me."

Three months later, in the great hall of the palace in Jhurat that was seldom open to the public, ordinary Cleo Churchill married His Excellency, the Sultan, in a traditional ceremony witnessed by hundreds in person and far more than that via the television cameras placed strategically throughout.

In your face, Brian, she thought at one point, because she was a tiny, tiny person.

Her hands were covered in henna, she was draped in breathlessly lovely scarves that made her look mysterious even in her own mirror, and the truth was that she felt like a complete stranger to herself as the typical Jhuratan wedding feast began. But then, she hadn't much liked the easily fooled, easily betrayed Cleo who'd stood there in such shock in Brian's condo, had she?

Now she was Khaled's wife. The chosen and beloved bride of a sultan, celebrated around the globe. Which meant she could never be *that* Cleo, pathetic and humiliated, again. *That* Cleo no longer existed. Only this one did.

"You must be having a laugh," her brand-new sister-in-law, Amira, had said when they'd told her the news not long after Khaled's proposal—not, Cleo reflected as she smiled politely at a cluster of wedding guests, that he had *proposed* so much as announced his intentions with every expectation of her obedience.

Amira's mouth had moved into something sulky when Khaled had murmured a phrase or two in silken Arabic. "A thousand congratulations," she'd said after a moment, her eyes so like her brother's, more silver than gray then, and fixed on Cleo intently, her mouth a petulant curve despite her words. "I hope this brings you everything you want."

Not exactly sincere happiness on her behalf, but then,

that had been thin on the ground. Cleo's family in Ohio had been baffled when she'd called to tell them the news and to invite them to come to Jhurat and meet the man who'd so enchanted her that she didn't intend to move back home at all.

"Are you *allowed* to come home?" her middle sister, Charity, had asked in her melodramatic way when Cleo had gotten her on the phone. "I've seen a lot of movies about this kind of thing—"

"She saw one Lifetime movie," Charity's long-suffering husband, Benji, had said on the extension.

"I *can* go wherever I want," Cleo had said, holding tight to her patience. "I don't *want* to go anywhere."

"It's all a bit of a whirlwind, isn't it?" her mother had asked after Khaled flew the whole family to Jhurat a month into their engagement, making Cleo tense even when her mother had smiled at her. "Like a fairy tale, with a palace and everything. Though it does seem a bit quick on the heels of all the unpleasantness last spring."

"This is certainly a flamboyant way to show Brian what he's missing," her sister Marnie had chimed in, her eyebrows so high on her forehead she'd looked perpetually surprised ever since she'd stepped off Khaled's private jet. "If you're willing to pay that kind of price."

"If you can't be happy for me, can you at least *try* to be polite?" Cleo had demanded, feeling wronged and isolated and annoyed at herself that she'd been so desperate for them to be happy about this.

"If you're happy, we're happy," her father had said then in his blustery way that had ended that topic of conversation, and the fact that he'd looked exactly the same as he always did—solid and decent and kind and *real,* even standing in a sumptuous palace a whole world away from home—had made Cleo something too close to teary.

"I think love at first sight is great," her best friend, Jessie, whom Cleo had known since they were in preschool together, had said via Skype from New Orleans. "But does it have to be *marriage* at first sight, too? Why not wait a little bit? What's the rush?"

"There's no rush."

"You hardly know him. I say that with love."

"I want this," she had gritted out, and it was a truth that echoed all the way down to her bones, making her hurt. "I want this more than I've ever wanted anything else."

"Okay." Jessie's eyes had been so worried, and Cleo had known what she'd say. "But you wanted Brian, too."

"Jessie," Cleo had said fiercely, "I need you to support me. Please? Can you just *support* me?"

And her best friend had nodded jerkily, then smiled wide and had never mentioned *waiting* or *Brian* again.

But all of that was nothing once the media got hold of the story, and Cleo's whirlwind romance in ancient Jhurat with its darkly handsome sultan claimed the imagination of people everywhere.

They combed through her life. They found embarrassing old pictures and splashed them online, on news shows, in those glossy magazines that made up things and printed them as breathless truth. They spoke to people who claimed to be old friends and talked about Cleo as if she were a vestal virgin claimed by a barbarian king. They made up stories and sassy nicknames, speculated, gossiped and called her the new Grace Kelly. The new Kate Middleton. The snider ones tutted and made dark predictions based as much on Jemima Khan's divorce from Imran Khan as on that humiliating picture of Cleo in a slutty Halloween costume her sophomore year in college that she was positive Brian had released to the tabloids. Perhaps in revenge, as no one seemed to care too much about his regrettable chapter in Cleo's life.

"This is awful," she'd complained to Khaled one night

at dinner, in a kind of wondering despair. "How do famous people bear it? How do you?"

"I didn't dress myself in a catsuit and parade about my undergraduate university," he'd said in that dry way that made her flush, that she wasn't certain was either amused or disapproving. Or both.

"That was a private picture." And she'd been hideously embarrassed that he'd seen it. That her parents had seen it. That *the entire world* had seen the effects of too much bravado and way too much beer. "But that doesn't seem to matter anymore."

"No," Khaled agreed. He'd taken her hand in his and played with it idly, as if he was unaware of the wildfire that even so innocuous a touch ignited within her when she knew very well he wasn't. "Most famous people stop reading about themselves and the fantasy lives the papers concoct for them." He'd met her gaze with that dark one of his as he lounged there across from her, so close and yet still so far out of reach that it made her stomach tighten. "I'd advise you to do the same."

"But it's all so invasive," she'd said, frowning. "It makes me feel *hunted*—"

His gaze had been so intense. Very nearly ferocious.

"It is unfair, of course," he'd said, and there'd been that harsh undertone to his voice then that she hadn't understood. "But this obsession the world has with my bride—with you—benefits Jhurat. If you are our Grace Kelly, that makes us Monaco, and that is precisely what we need. You understand this, I hope?"

Duty governs everything I do, he'd told her once before, and that had hung between them then, sending a kind of chill straight down her spine.

"Of course," she'd assured him. "Of course I understand."

Because Cleo wanted this. She wanted the goddamned

fantasy. She wanted sleek and elegant Cleo Churchill who'd bewitched a sultan—the woman she read about in the papers. She wanted happiness and fairy tales and unrealistic bliss. She *deserved* it.

"Don't you look fancy!" Marnie had exclaimed when she'd seen the way Cleo dressed for dinner in Jhurat, and again, not in a way that was precisely complimentary.

"I'm marrying a sultan," Cleo had bitten out, sharper and ruder than she'd meant to sound, trying hard not to fidget and pull at the chic dress she wore instead of the cargo pants and T-shirts she'd lived in at home. "I should look the part, don't you think?"

It hadn't been lost on her that Khaled wouldn't permit her to *let herself go,* if only because he provided her with a wardrobe. Or that, because he told her she was beautiful, she wanted to be exactly that for him.

"You should look like *you,*" Charity had replied fiercely, but Cleo had tuned them both out.

She *deserved* this. All of it. And particularly Khaled.

She wanted to believe that most of all.

It had been no great hardship to listen to Margery, the social secretary Khaled had hired for her, who had ushered Cleo through all her interviews and had crafted her image—and her carefully edited story of who she was and how she'd come to attract the notice of her powerful fiancé in the first place—to her soon-to-be husband's precise specifications.

The ravenous world—hungry for stories that ended happily ever after in castles with good-looking princes or kings or even sultans gazing adoringly at ordinary girls from next-door places like Ohio, just as everyone dreamed, Margery assured her—ate it all up with a spoon.

"You look so sophisticated!" Jessie had cried one night a few weeks before the wedding. They'd been on a Skype call after a charity ball in Paris that Khaled had wanted to attend for the press attention alone, and if her best friend's expression wasn't quite as thrilled as her tone of voice, Cleo told herself it was simply the computer connection. The long hours Jessie had been putting in at her law firm. Nothing more. "Like a movie star!"

"I've never felt more beautiful," Cleo had told her, and it was true.

Because when she looked in the mirror, she was glowing. With happiness. With disbelief that this was happening to her. With excitement about the life that lay before her, gleaming as brightly as the jewels Khaled lavished upon her or the smiles he parceled out like rare and precious gifts.

With that happily ever after that the whole world was suddenly as invested in as she was. That she was certain she'd earned.

And she was the only one who knew that Khaled hadn't touched her again as he had that night in his courtyard, or in that hall outside the suite of rooms she still inhabited.

"We will save something for the marriage bed, I think," he'd told her when she'd tried to move their nightly kisses somewhere hotter that same night in Paris, after spending so much of the evening dancing in his arms in front of all the cameras.

"What if I don't want to wait?" she'd asked, wild and very nearly furious with wanting him. Desperate with needing him.

He'd run his finger down her nose and smiled, though there was an edge in it.

"You will do it anyway," he'd told her softly.

"Because you say so?"

"Because I wish it," he'd replied, which she'd thought was pretty much the same thing. "Is that not enough?"

It had been an agonizing three months, Cleo thought now as the wedding feast roared on around her, but the waiting was over at last. Khaled might have been deep in conversation with emissaries from other countries, the dignitaries and financiers she understood he needed to lure to Jhurat and could in a different way than before, thanks to the worldwide interest their wedding had generated, but soon enough they would be on their own. He would take her from the palace and she would finally, *finally* be his in every possible way.

That same fire she'd tasted that night three months ago simmered in her at the thought, making her cheeks heat, making her stomach clench in delicious anticipation, making her feel hungry and wild despite all the eyes trained on her.

Almost as if he'd left them both unfulfilled deliberately.

"Where are we going?" she asked when Khaled finally took her by the hand and led her from the banquet to the sound of so many cheers, though the truth was she didn't care at all as long as he was with her.

"You will see when we get there," Khaled told her, and then he smiled down at her in a way that made her quiver deep inside, all that dark intent on his fierce face, all of his focus on her, at last. *At last.* "Though I must warn you, *wife,* that I doubt you will see much at all outside my bed."

CHAPTER FOUR

KHALED WAS PREPARED to give in to this madness—this wild hunger he knew better than to indulge—for exactly one week.

"Take more time," his father had told him in one of his lucid moments, so few and far between these days. "All marriages need time to recover from the onslaught of all that wedding nonsense. That takes more than a week."

"I appreciate that, Father," he'd said, though the old man's gaze had already been losing focus as he'd spoken, and his father was possibly the last man on earth whose advice Khaled would ever take regarding such matters. "But a week is all the time I can allow."

He had carved out seven days and decided that would be that.

Because the way to craft the kind of marriage he required could not involve this simmering heat that danced between them, making it harder to concentrate than it should have been. Making him question his own decisions. Making him *feel* things he didn't want to feel. He had courted her deliberately, rushed her to the altar, made her the very picture of fairy-tale romance for all the world to sigh over—but now it was done and it was time to change direction. Reap the rewards of the attention their wedding had brought to Jhurat and distance himself from his too-tempting bride before he repeated the mistakes his own parents had made.

But first, these seven stolen days. To pretend he was a different man. To indulge his ravenous hunger for the pretty American with the wide honey eyes he'd made his wife. To watch her fall apart like that again, over and over, until he was glutted.

He'd been selfish enough to drag her into his world. He was selfish enough to taste her the way he wanted, to lose himself in her for a time, then return to reality and set the necessary boundaries.

But there was obviously some part of him that wondered.

"I shouldn't take the whole week," he'd muttered to Nasser after yet another conference call with a trio of big oil kingpins from Texas some weeks back, whose hearty twangs and ingrained dismissiveness had made Khaled feel murderous—not that it would prevent him from inviting each and every one of them to his pageant of a wedding anyway. "I can hardly spare a day."

"What is that proverb?" Nasser had asked in his mild way. "'Marriage is like a castle besieged—those who are on the outside wish to get in—'"

"'And those who are on the inside wish to get out,'" Khaled had finished for him impatiently. "So you see my point."

"I confess, Your Excellency, I was thinking of your long-suffering bride-to-be," Nasser had replied, wisely keeping that smirk in his voice from his face.

Khaled knew he shouldn't do this. He even knew that he was lying to himself. The astonishing truth was that his hunger for this woman, his ceaseless need, had reached the breaking point.

If he didn't have her soon, he thought he might hurt someone.

But one week was all he'd allow himself.

One week to slake this consuming, destructive lust that had haunted him since the night she'd gone to pieces in his arms in the courtyard of his own palace, shocking him to the core and awakening that terrible need inside him that had only grown sharper since then. One week to get his fill of this woman he wanted more than was at all wise, so he could move on with his responsibilities without this *hunger* gnawing at him at the most inopportune moments.

One week to pretend he could let himself love her, when he knew he couldn't. When he knew there was only duty. Only and ever his duty.

He'd given all of his Western allies ample reason to invest their resources in Jhurat by making his wedding the culmination of a thousand romantic fantasies, and his country now seemed accessible and desirable instead of exotic and frightening. He could get back to work on what mattered: saving Jhurat from itself. His duty was what mattered, not his marriage.

One week is all I need, he told himself fiercely as they climbed into the helicopter and set out into the beautiful twilight desolation of the desert, leaving the jutting spires of the capital city and the wild cheering from their wedding celebration behind, *and I will conquer this* thing *that claws at me whenever I look at her.*

It was only sex, he reasoned. The sex he'd deliberately withheld, because he'd hoped to control it. And her. It was *only* sex, he told himself now, because anything else was a danger to them both.

Sex and impossible chemistry and that polished gold gaze of hers that pricked at him, even when, like now, she wasn't even looking at him. Sleep had claimed her as the helicopter raced over the great desert into the coming night, and Khaled assured himself it was the promise of sex alone that made his heart beat faster the closer they came to his family's private oasis, hidden away in the golden, shifting, treacherous hills of sand that were his birthright.

It wasn't her flawless skin, only partially concealed by the feminine, entrancing scarves she wore. It wasn't the henna that marked her as surely as he wanted to mark her, claim her. It wasn't that slender beauty of hers in the dress she wore, which he knew would grace the cover of a hundred magazines and still not quite capture what fascinated him most about her. Her clever gaze. That disrespectful scowl. Her soft mouth. The smoke and rasp of her surprisingly sensual laughter. The innate grace she'd had all along, hidden beneath her grubby Western clothes and tied-back hair, waiting only to be called forth. Celebrated.

Made his.

He gathered her in his arms when the helicopter landed, holding her high against his chest as he made his way to the large tent that had been prepared for them. He felt like a conqueror. Like a king. As if he'd won her in a long, pitched battle. She stirred as he strode through the camp, those eyes as golden as his desert blinking up at him, her pretty mouth curving into a smile as she recognized him.

It was as if she thought he was safe. Khaled wished that were true.

But there would only be this week, and then they would play their appointed roles, and he knew it was the best way. The only way. Hadn't he seen his parents try and fail to mix duty with desire? It caused nothing but destruction.

"Where are we?" she asked, her voice a rough little whisper that he felt like a caress.

"It is an oasis. It is much more private than the palace. We'll have it to ourselves for the week."

He didn't try to contain the heat he felt at that idea, and he knew he needed to burn this all away. He needed to wrestle it into submission. He needed to be in control.

Of it. Of her. Of all the things that had happened since his sister had jumped in front of her car.

Because he had nothing but this country, could want nothing but this country, could focus on nothing but this country. It was the only thing he allowed himself to love, and he knew too well what happened when men in his position tried to love anything else. He'd watched it play out in front of him throughout his childhood. He'd lived with the results. With his mother's abandonment of him, of Amira, of the world, because she loved her own misery and broken heart more than her family—and what it had done to his father.

He would not let history repeat itself. He would take this week—and then he would put Cleo in her proper place and keep her there, no matter what happened. No matter how he felt.

Not that he *felt* anything, he told himself sternly. That was for lesser men.

"I've never seen an oasis before," Cleo said after a moment, seemingly unaware of the wars he fought and wasn't at all sure he won inside. "But this is exactly what I imagined one would look like."

Khaled was too consumed with her to look around, and besides, he knew what he'd see. The layers of trees that ringed the soft aquamarine waters, date palms and peaches, olives and figs, lit up with a hundred lanterns tonight to greet the sultan and his new bride. The small collection of tents with the most sprawling in the center, marked with flaming torches at the entrance, which was where he headed now. And around them, nothing but the deep quiet of the desert sands and the riot of galaxies above them in the night sky.

As though they were all alone in the world. The whole universe.

That howled in him like power. Like thick, enduring need.

Khaled pushed through the tent's heavy flap, and only when they were inside did he place Cleo on her feet. With a gentleness that spoke to a level of emotional attachment he refused to admit he felt. Because he couldn't.

She swayed slightly, he reached out a hand to steady her, and then he watched her face intently as she looked around in undisguised wonder. Tapestries flowed from the high ceiling down to the ground, carpets stretched lush and deep across the ground and the tent was furnished with a seating area, two dressing areas and the wide, inviting bed that stood in the center.

She stared at it for a moment too long.

"This is beautiful," she said in that same soft voice. "Like something in a dream."

"It is basic," Khaled said with a shrug. Humor lit her gaze when she looked at him again, and she smiled. He was surprised when he did, too.

"But then, you are His Excellency, the Sultan of Jhurat," she said, that laughter that undid him thick in her voice, bright in her golden eyes, as sweet as honey from his own bees. "Accustomed to far greater luxuries than this."

"Did you eat?" he asked coolly, trying to leash that animal in him that wanted nothing more than to throw her down and feast on her until it'd had its fill.

Your fill or one week, that treacherous voice inside him taunted him. *I wonder which will come first?*

"Eat?" she echoed, as if she'd never heard the word.

"I didn't see you touch any of the food at the wedding feast," he said gently, when he didn't want *gentle.* When he wanted nothing at all but her. Hot and hard and *his,* irrevocably. "You must be hungry."

"I'm not."

"Cleo," he said calmly. Deliberately. "Heed me, please. You will need your strength."

He watched desire heat her cheeks, make her golden eyes gleam, and his smile turned darker. Harder.

"Maybe," she said, as bold as she was nervous, and he thought she might kill him after all, this creature who shouldn't have appealed to him at all. Who was so responsive to him that it very nearly hurt to remember it, and yet he was suddenly certain he'd thought of nothing else since. "But I need you more."

He reached over and pulled her scarves from her, one by one, unwrapping each layer of her like the gift she was, listening as her breath caught and then came faster, watching as her skin pinkened. Feeling it all like her delicate hands on his sex, making him so hard he ached.

There was no room left for teasing.

"Be careful," he warned her quietly, the intensity of his hunger making his voice sound lethal in the quiet tent. "When I touch you this time, I won't stop. I won't even try."

She swallowed hard. Her eyes were like the dizzying stars above, wide and bright. And he couldn't think of a single thing he'd ever wanted more than her touch. Her taste. Her beautiful cries as she wrapped herself around him.

Her. *His wife.*

His in every way there was.

"Khaled," she whispered as if she felt the same. Needy. Hungry. Near to insane with it. "If you don't touch me right now I think I might kill you, and that would make this an embarrassingly short marriage." Her mouth curved. "And I'd end up *detained* after all."

He laughed. And then he stopped trying to pretend he was anything but wild where this woman was concerned. He stopped trying to cling to some notion of propriety.

She was his, fierce and inappropriate and lovely beyond measure. It was time.

Khaled thought he might have growled when he pulled her close and set his mouth to hers, and he gloried in it.

He was claiming her at last.

Khaled's mouth was hard and perfect on hers, hot and wild.

Like fate, Cleo thought; *like he's mine*—and then she burst into a delirious fever of shuddering heat, and she met him.

This time, she expected the punch, the blast of flame and need. They'd kissed in these past three months, but it had never burst into that same bright white fire the way it had that first time. It had never gone supernova again, because Khaled had always, always, maintained his iron control. He'd always set her away from him far sooner than she'd wanted. He'd always pulled back, shut it down, told her he'd wanted them to wait.

Always.

It took her one hot, slick kiss, then another, to realize with a deep, delicious thrill that this time, Khaled wasn't holding back.

One of his hands slid around and into her hair, anchoring her for his pleasure as his mouth moved over hers, tongue and teeth and all of that dizzying, heart-pounding passion.

That bright white heat. That impossible flame. That addicting blaze so hot it almost hurt, so hot she was sure it would burn her alive, and she couldn't imagine wanting anything more.

When he broke away, Cleo let out a small sound of disappointment, and he laughed against her mouth.

It was a sound filled with deep male confidence, power and certainty, and it made Cleo melt.

"These have been the longest months of my life," he

muttered, so low she wondered for a moment if he even knew he was speaking out loud. And then his voice went even rougher. "This is not what I had planned."

Cleo didn't know what he meant and with his mouth against her neck, she didn't care. She wound her arms around his gorgeous shoulders and pressed herself against the length of his magnificent body, and this time, he let her.

He let out a sound like a growl, not for the first time, and then he swept her up into his arms again. The room spun, drunken and beautiful, like the perfect roller coaster. She had only a wild, dizzy impression of the rich colors throughout the tent, the candles in glass lanterns spilling out all of that golden light, and her brand-new husband's hard, fierce face, dark and intent as he gazed down at her.

He was hers. He was finally *hers*.

And then she was on her back on that big, wide bed and he was coming over her, pinning her to the soft mattress with all of his ferocious heat and power, and she loved it.

"I was going to take my time," he told her, his voice harsh, but she knew what that glittering, edgy gleam in his dark eyes meant.

She could feel him, hard and demanding against her, and she shivered. She was too hot, too molten, too needy, and she wasn't sure he'd ever be close enough.

"I think you took your time," she managed to say, with only the faintest trace of her former laughter, because this was all far too intense now. "Every day of the past three months."

He muttered something much darker and then he moved over her, pulling the voluminous skirt of her wedding dress up with him, baring her legs and her thighs and then even higher.

God, the way she wanted him. The way she *needed* him. She'd never felt anything like it. She couldn't imagine anyone had.

Khaled held her gaze as he reached down and held the hungry center of her need in his hand.

It was as if she wasn't wearing those silly scraps of lace at all. She felt the heat of his hand like a jolt of lightning, setting her on fire, and he did nothing for one heartbeat and another but hold her. But wait. Until her hips started reaching for him of their own accord, rocking into that hard palm of his, and she was powerless to stop it.

She didn't *want* to stop it.

"Beautiful," he muttered, and then he pushed the edge of her panties aside and traced the greedy button beneath, and it took Cleo a shuddering breath to realize that the keening sound she heard, edgy and haunted and deliciously needy, came from *her*. That he'd undone her so easily, with a single touch.

The way he had once before.

"Khaled," she began, though she had no idea what she meant to say.

Maybe it was more of a prayer, and he only laughed, bracing himself over her with one hand in a fist near her head. And then he twisted his wrist and sent two fingers stroking deep inside her.

And Cleo simply went mad.

She arched into him, wanton and mindless, without a single thought for anything that wasn't this.

Here. Now. *Him.*

"Now, Cleo," he ordered her in that matter-of-fact, authoritative way that made her burn, as if he was the lord and master of her body as well as his country, and she believed it. She felt it. "I cannot wait much longer."

And she obeyed.

Again and again, she obeyed, shaking and shuddering and falling apart all around him.

And when she came back to herself, when she could breathe again, he was braced above her, the hardest part of him nudged up against her melting softness. Her heart thumped too hard in her chest, and she was caught in all the dark, male heat in his gaze.

"Please," she whispered, and he thrust deep.

So deep. So perfect. Long and slick and hotter than simple fire.

She didn't know if she groaned or he did. She didn't care.

Cleo reached up and held on to him, curling her legs around his hips, and watched his fiercely beautiful face as he set a torturously slow and devilish pace. One deliberately slow thrust, then another, until Cleo was shaking against him, as needy and demanding and wild as if she hadn't already shattered into pieces.

"Again," he ordered her.

"I can't," she hissed at him, a broken whisper, and the fire inside her raged on.

"Never lie to me, little one," he whispered, and then he took her mouth with his, wicked and carnal and certain while he thrust so deep below, and she was lost all over again.

And this time, when she burst into too many scattered points of light to remain whole or even herself, he called out her name and followed her.

Cleo didn't know how much later it was when Khaled roused himself and slowly peeled her dress from her body. The lanterns still danced with light, and the tent felt hushed all around them, as if the way he looked at her then was sacred.

And if there was that yearning thing in her, dark and deep and lodged behind her heart, that wanted it to be sacred and then some, she ignored it and made herself smile at him. This formidable man who stood at the edge of the vast bed and stripped down in front of her.

Her husband. Her lover. *Hers.*

Cleo's mouth went dry. He was even more beautiful without his clothes on, all those smooth, hard planes and lean muscles like poured metal in the flickering light. How could she want him again when she wasn't sure she'd recovered from having him once already? But her body stirred, that fist low in her belly clenching tight and hot all over again.

"Do you swim?" he asked.

His voice was still rough, and Cleo frowned at him, not understanding why the question bothered her.

"I do," she said. She propped herself up on her elbows, still wearing the lace panties he'd shoved to one side and the matching lace bra that he'd only revealed afterward, when he'd helped her out of her wedding dress. Something hot and odd twisted around inside her, like a too-sharp band of metal around that low heat, and she didn't know why. "I was a lifeguard at the town pool for at least five summers after I turned sixteen."

"Thank goodness. I feel safer already."

Cleo wanted to smile back at him, but there was that yearning place inside her and the sharp thing besides, and she couldn't.

"I never thought my husband would be a stranger to me," she said without thinking it through, then froze.

Khaled stared at her for a moment, imperious and ferocious, and Cleo forced herself to sit up. To stop lolling about like a satiated sex kitten when she felt so ragged and unwieldy inside.

"I told you that you should eat," he said quietly after a moment, his tone so even and mild that it made her flush with embarrassment at what her own had been. "Hunger affects the mood."

"I'm not a child," she said crossly.

He was magnificently nude as he stalked toward her,

looking like a warrior god clad only in the force of his will and the candlelight from the glass-paned lanterns, and that thing in her flipped over. Then twisted in on itself.

What are you doing? she demanded. *This* is *happily ever after.* And when he touched her, she knew it was true. When he touched her, there was no room for anything but happily ever after in him.

"Come," he said when he was before her, a wall of perfect masculinity. "There are better things to do tonight than pick fights from thin air, Cleo. Let me show you."

She thought that was the kindest she'd ever seen him, and she didn't know why it made her want to curl up in a ball and sob.

He reached down and scooped her up again, high against his chest again, and she found her face entirely too close to his. All that fire and awe mixed inside her, making her feel jittery. Making her want things she couldn't even name.

"I can walk."

"I don't want you to walk or you would be walking."

"And everything must be what you want or the world will fly apart at the seams?"

But that strange heaviness was already spiraling out of her as he held her against the furnacelike heat of his bare chest, and he only raised his brows as he gazed down at her.

"Of course," he said mildly. "I am the sultan."

She shouldn't find his arrogance so comforting, Cleo thought. But she did. She slid an arm around his shoulders as he carried her out into the soft night again.

"Won't someone see us?" she asked when they were out beneath the stars again, so many of them it was hard to look.

"And if they do?"

"You're naked! I might as well be!"

"They are trained not to look when they know they shouldn't," he replied, amused. "Unlike you, Cleo, they prefer not to risk my wrath."

When he set her down, it was in a three-sided tent at the edge of the gently murmuring pool of water in the center of the oasis. The tent was lit with more lanterns, piled high with comfortable lounging chairs, towels and pillows and rugs, and there were trays of food set out on low tables.

"Eat," he ordered her. "Then you and I will swim beneath the moon. And I will make you scream my name into the night until you are hoarse."

Khaled smiled then, glancing up at her as he threw himself down beside the table and stretched out, a vision of naked male perfection, proud and fierce and hers.

Hers, Cleo reminded herself. He was *hers,* even if that felt different in the execution than she'd expected it to in all these long months of daydreaming.

"And what if I want to make *you* scream?" she asked, but she moved to other side of the table and lowered herself down before the trays of food, pita breads and dipping things, fruits and salads and cuts of meats and cheeses, something baked to a deep golden crisp and smelling savory. She realized as she did that she was starving.

"You are welcome to try," Khaled said, sounding amused as he fixed himself a plate. "But if it is some kind of competition, you should understand that I do not care to lose."

Cleo took a big bite of pita bread, sighing at the airy, doughy taste. She dipped it into a bowl of handmade hummus, then popped a few olives into her mouth for good measure. Perfect, of course. As was everything that was his.

As this marriage would be. As it was already.

"Does that mean you don't lose? Or that you're a sore loser when you do?"

His smile took on that darker edge that made her heartbeat slow down and hit harder.

"Is this what I have to look forward to in my marriage?" he asked in a soft tone, but she heard the steel beneath. "A disrespectful wife who pokes at me at every opportunity?"

"Only when she's hungry," Cleo said, and smiled. Then let out a breath when his hard mouth curved slightly, as though she'd dodged something dangerous there in that otherwise cheerful tent.

She told herself it didn't matter that they were still strangers in so many ways. They weren't the first people in the world to marry without knowing each other's every private thought and they wouldn't be the last, either. And what good was it to know someone, anyway? They could be lying. She'd learned that firsthand. She'd thought she knew every last thing there was to know about Brian because she'd dated him for years, only to find out how wrong she was a mere two weeks before her wedding.

Thinking about Brian here, now, felt like an obscenity. Cleo shoved it away.

What mattered was this *thing* that wound between her and Khaled and around them, tying them together. She could feel it in the air. Lust and longing, recognition and discovery, and, yes, love, she thought, new and raw and different from anything she'd ever felt before. And she couldn't think of a single reason he would have married her if he didn't feel the same—though, she rationalized as they ate their meal in a silence she assured herself was companionable, he was a very closed-off man. A powerful man with tremendous responsibilities. She couldn't expect him to be emotional and accessible.

And when he touched her, it was magic.

Did there have to be more than that?

Later, they floated in the silky dark water with the moon bright and full above them. He trapped her near one of the edges and took her mouth with that same restrained ferocity that made every part of her skin prickle in delight. They were both naked and sleek in the night, the water only a degree or two cooler than the embrace of the night all around them, and he simply lifted her up and slid inside her, making her gasp.

This time, he wasn't slow. He took her hard and deep, with a possessiveness and dark need, and she reveled in it. His arms were like bands around her, the hard length of him a deep and wondrous fire within her.

He laughed when she moaned, and then he bent her backward, making Cleo feel as graceful as a dancer in the water and beneath the moon—then he found her breast with his hot, dangerous mouth, and her moan turned into something much needier. Sensation streaked through her, from the tight peak he teased with his lips and his teeth and his tongue to the place where they were joined, where he filled her again and again and tore her apart with every sweet, sure thrust.

"I can't..." she gritted out.

"My name," he ordered her, and bit gently on her nipple, and she shuddered around him, a kind of wild, red joy wrapping around her and pulling her taut. "Say it, Cleo. Scream it if you must."

And she couldn't keep herself from obeying him then. She didn't want to do anything but obey him. His name was like a cry, like a prayer, to the moon and the water and the oasis around them. To the desert.

To this man who was her husband. Whom she suspected she loved already and recklessly, far more than was safe. Much less wise. Whom she thought she'd loved almost from the first moment she'd seen him, striding before her like a fierce god in the street.

But when she came back to earth, he was waiting, still so hot and hard inside her, and the look on his beautiful face was stark with passion. His gray eyes gleamed with that edgy need that still raced through her.

"Again, I think," he said. "I don't believe that was quite loud enough. The trees still stand, do they not?"

"I don't like to scream," she whispered.

"You will," he promised her, lust and amusement and the whole world in his dark gaze.

"I don't know how."

His mouth curved, and he began to move again, slow this time. Sweet and lethal and perfect, and her eyes drifted closed.

"Practice makes perfect," he said.

And then he showed her what he meant.

CHAPTER FIVE

BACK IN THE palace, Cleo's days as the sultan's wife were full.

She took lessons in Arabic, Jhuratan history, formal protocol and etiquette for part of each day, then spent the rest involved with the many charity organizations that clamored for the attention of the sultan's brand-new bride. There were the endless wardrobe fittings, scrupulously polite meetings with the wives of visiting dignitaries and visit after visit to all the places that the sultan deemed worthy of his notice and patronage.

This was what the good life looked like, she told herself. This was her unrealistic fairy tale, and she had every intention of excelling at the duties that came along with it.

"You are very popular with the people," Khaled had told her when she'd indicated, long weeks after their magical time in the oasis, that she wasn't exactly thrilled with her role as no more than his distant appendage. He'd studied her as if she was as much a mystery to him as he was still to her—and then he'd pulled her close to taste her mouth, making a sound as if he'd meant to resist her, but couldn't. "And it costs so little to smile and wave, Cleo. Does it not?"

Khaled believed she could do it—and because he did, so did she.

This particular afternoon she'd toured a home for abandoned children, had tried out her halting Arabic while cutting a ribbon outside a newly constructed school and was now frowning down at the schedule for her next month of duties. Margery, her starchy social secretary, had handed it to her in the backseat of the armored car that whisked them back toward the palace.

"I can't do all of these benefits." Cleo glared at the blocks of time in the grid, all the entries filled in with Margery's pinched block letters, which infuriated her in ways she'd spent a long time these past weeks cautioning herself not to indulge, because she was *happy*. Ever freaking after. As planned. "There's something almost every single night."

Beside her, Margery projected an air of condescension with only the faintest lift of her brow, something Cleo had tolerated a great deal better before her wedding. Cleo didn't much care for Margery, she realized then. Not that anyone had asked her.

"Your office—" by this Margery meant herself "—has already sent your gracious acceptance to all of the noted events, my lady. It would be considered curious, at best, to pull out now."

Curious, Cleo had learned, was Margery's code word for "completely unacceptable." And "we won't do it your way no matter who you're married to." It was a word she used a lot.

"I can miss a dinner with my husband every now and again," Cleo said, not sure why she suddenly felt gripped by something much too intense for a discussion about scheduling, especially when her dinners with Khaled had been so few and far between lately, and they always ended up naked and wild and not eating anyway, "but not every night. He wouldn't like it."

She hated that she felt compelled to use Khaled as a bargaining chip. That she felt compelled to bargain.

Margery didn't look up from the folder she always held

before her like a shield, forever making notes she didn't
share with Cleo.

"His Excellency approved your schedule personally,"
Margery said coolly.

Cleo blinked at that unexpected slap, but by now she
knew better than to betray her feelings any further than
she already had. This new life of hers was divided into the
very few private spaces where she could do and say and
think as she liked, and everywhere else—and that division
had never seemed so stark or unforgiving as it did now.

Margery, she understood suddenly, worked for the palace. For Khaled.

Not for her. How had she failed to notice that before
now?

"What part of you is the sultan and which part of you
is the man?" she'd asked Khaled while they were still in
the oasis. They had been lying lazily in that tent near the
sheer blue murmur of the pool, listening to the rustle of the
palms and the whisper of the wind through the sands all
around them. She had been on top of him, with him still
deep inside her, their most recent storm just over.

The next one had been building, even then. It always
was.

"They are the same thing," he'd said, and she'd told
herself that hadn't been *warning* she heard in his voice.
That he hadn't sounded *ravaged,* merely intense. "Indistinguishable. The man makes no decisions that do not ben-
efit the sultan."

Cleo had traced the mesmerizing trail of dark hair that
dusted his chest with her fingertips. "And is the sultan as
concerned about the needs of the man?"

She'd been joking. But he'd jackknifed up and set her
aside, and then wrapped one of the thick towels around
him when he went to stand in the tent's opening, the hot

desert sun cascading over him, gilding him in all that gold. Making him that much more beautiful.

And tortured, too, she'd seen when he'd turned back to her.

"There is only the sultan, Cleo," he'd said in a dark tone. "There is only Jhurat."

"Was that Jhurat who just made me scream?" she'd asked lightly, certain she could tease him out of this mood. She'd been getting better at it every day. "For the third time today? I thought that was you."

His mouth had twisted, his dark eyes had flashed and she'd thought he might unleash that temper of his—some part of her had welcomed it, for reasons she'd been unwilling to probe too deeply—but he'd only shaken his head.

"Remember that I warned you," he'd said, too quietly. "Remember that I never pretended otherwise. Remember this, Cleo."

But she'd forgotten it the moment he'd pulled her to her feet again, the way she always forgot everything when he touched her. That she hardly knew him. That she'd married the fantasy as much as she'd married him. He'd taken her mouth—and then the rest of her—with that barely restrained ferocity that made her feel more alive, more beautiful, more wild and more cherished than she'd ever been in her life.

She remembered it now, and something cold moved through her, oily and slippery, but she knew better than to show anything while she was under the watchful eye of her secretary.

"Very well, then, Margery," she murmured instead, folding her hands and gazing out the window as if she was perfectly unbothered. "Thank you."

It turned out Cleo was very good at acting perfectly composed and quietly confident. Or so the papers—which she couldn't buy for herself when she was always under some kind of disapproving surveillance or another, yet supportive Jessie scanned and emailed her now and again anyway—claimed. Khaled's "ordinary queen" was a cool and stylish newlywed, she read in all those articles that talked about her as if they knew her personally. Polite and calm no matter what, as if she'd been born to her brand-new station. Graceful and inscrutable.

It was all exactly how she'd wanted it, in the papers. She was Khaled's queen, not a woman someone wholly unremarkable like Brian would throw over. She'd started over as if from scratch, completely erasing her entire previous life.

If only she felt she fit into her new one better.

Especially because, now that the wedding was over, what the papers speculated about was whether or not she was pregnant—and if that was the slightly less romantic, and certainly less flattering, reason for her breathlessly quick engagement to a man who had never looked even remotely inclined toward matrimony before. "Does the sultan have a baby on the way?" the headlines asked. "Is that a bump behind Cleo's coat?" Was this all a game of smoke and mirrors from the start?

It occurred to her as the armored car navigated its way through the crowded center of the city that she had no idea what Khaled thought about having children. That there were any number of things she'd simply…neglected to ask him, so caught up had she been in the whirlwind of their engagement.

In her total commitment to living this fantasy to the fullest.

She'd never regretted that before. She found she did now. More deeply than she wanted to admit.

Margery droned on about the following day's duties. Cleo tuned her out. *Do you know Khaled at all?* a dark little voice whispered inside her head. *Do you want to?*

Because the man she'd thought she'd married wouldn't have signed off on an entire month of never seeing her without a single reservation. Without so much as discussing it with her first.

But then, there were a lot of things Khaled didn't find it necessary to discuss with her.

Cleo had expected to move in to his bedroom—with him—when they'd returned from their week in the desert. She hadn't been able to hide her stunned disappointment when he'd directed her to remain where she was instead, in her suite in a different wing of the palace from his as though she was still a guest instead of his wife.

"We won't sleep in the same room?" she'd asked, astonished. She'd found herself powerfully addicted to his touch by then, after a week spent so close to him she knew how his skin tasted at different times of day, could feel the weight of his strong arms slung across her, holding her close, even when they weren't touching. Which was seldom.

"I am thinking only of your comfort," he'd told her smoothly—but even then, so sated and dazzled by him, she'd wondered if there was too much darkness in his gray gaze as he kept it level on hers. And he hadn't been touching her then, had he? "I keep odd hours. I wouldn't wish to disturb your sleep."

"I like it when you disturb my sleep," Cleo had replied, frowning at him. She'd been thinking of that very morning in their tent, sometime before dawn, when she'd woken to find him already moving into her, waking her and taking her in the same thrilling moment.

The beauty of it had still thrummed in her all those hours later, a live wire of sensation and desire. That perfect, glorious, dizzying fit that was only theirs, as if they'd been created for each other. How could he want to lose that?

Khaled's mouth had crooked to one side, his gaze had

gleamed in that way she'd discovered meant he wanted her, but he'd only shaken his head—the sultan once more, she'd thought, instead of her dark, passionate lover. "I suspect I will find ways to disturb you in that way more often that I should, no matter where we sleep."

Later, she'd told herself there hadn't been a raw note in his voice when he'd said that, very much as if he wished he could fight it. Fight *her*. She'd told herself she was simply overemotional after such an intense honeymoon, as anyone would be.

And besides, he came to her in the night, almost every night. He was a commanding force, tearing her into a thousand pieces again and again and then disappearing before sunrise.

"No one else will ever touch you," he'd whispered to her hoarsely in the hot, slick dark, more than once. "I am not a civilized man, Cleo."

"I don't want civilized," she'd whispered back, and when he drove into her with all that power and glory that only grew deeper every time they tested it, she hadn't been sure she even knew what civilized *was*. She certainly hadn't cared.

She'd thought that was passion. Need. Even love, raw and wild.

She'd thought it was enough.

The mornings were harder, because she woke alone. The desert sun rose hot and pitiless over the old city, and the moment Karima appeared in her bedroom to start her day, Cleo had to perform her brand-new role. The wife of the sultan never had days off.

This *was* the dream, she told herself. Her perfect fantasy. This was what she'd wanted.

The daily breakfasts had disappeared the moment they'd returned from the oasis. Their habitual dinners had stopped being nightly some time back, it was true—but there had always been reasonable excuses for that. Khaled ran a country, after all. He was legitimately busy. How could she possibly complain?

Missing a scheduled dinner, however, wasn't the same as removing those dinners from the schedule altogether. Cleo mulled that over the rest of the day, as she tended to some official correspondence in the graceful office in the public wing of the palace that Margery had decorated and now ran and yet everyone called hers.

She turned it around and around in her head as she ate her dinner on a tray in her rooms, sitting out on the balcony that overlooked the courtyard and remembering that night out there with Khaled, when he'd first touched her and shattered her without even removing her clothes. Then proposed. How had they gone from that place to this?

How could she not know?

Late that night, Khaled lay sprawled next to her, his skin so hot against hers and his breath still ragged, and Cleo told herself that questioning him could wait. She wanted to enjoy him. This. She wanted to bask in him as if they had all the time in the world, the way they had at the oasis.

He'd walked into her room earlier without so much as a knock, the way he always did. He'd stood for a moment and stared at her as if she'd summoned him and he was powerless to resist her—and furious about it. He always did that, too. He'd pulled her up from where she'd been reading on the chaise near the windows with a simple curl of his hard hand around her neck, and then he'd been kissing her before she could draw breath. As fierce and as all-consuming as that first kiss. As every kiss. That fire between them blazing on, unchanged and untempered by the passage of time.

None of it was logical. None of it made sense. She'd had sex before and she'd believed it was good sex, but it had never been an *inferno* like this. It had never battered at her, changing everything, making her worry she might disappear into him forever and worse, that she might not care if she did.

And now they were lying there in the dim light of her bedroom, he was beside her, which was exactly where she wanted him most, and it would be childish to complain about not seeing *more* of him, wouldn't it? The last thing she wanted was for him to think she was petulant—or that she couldn't handle the realities of his life. This fantastical, fairy-tale life. *Their life.*

"The entire world thinks I'm pregnant," she told him, blurting the words out recklessly before she was tempted to say something else that might ruin the moment. He stirred beside her, the hand that had been toying idly with her hair—now so long it reached the center of her back, the way he'd told her again and again he liked it—going still.

"Define 'the entire world,' please."

She'd thought he would laugh, and now wished she'd stayed silent and enjoyed basking in him instead. "Perhaps not the whole world. Just its most appalling tabloid papers."

"Did we not agree that you were not to read the papers? Unless your secretary presents specific articles to you for your review?"

He didn't sound particularly annoyed, though her stomach was tight and *His Excellency approved,* Margery had said.

"We did not agree on that, in fact," she replied with a flash of temper. "You advised me not to read them, and I took your opinion under due consideration."

"'Advised' you?" Cleo didn't trust that light tone he used, or the way he continued to hold himself so very still. "I was unaware that I operated in an advisory capacity."

"Because you aren't often asked for advice?"

"Because most of what I say becomes law even as I say

it." He shifted next to her, and if she was a better person, she thought then, she wouldn't allow herself to get lost in the play of the muscles in his arms, across his chest. "I don't allow that filth in the palace and you can hardly stop a motorcade at a news agent's on the street without making the evening news. How could you possibly read the papers?"

"I didn't realize that I was actually *forbidden* from reading anything I chose," she said, trying to make her voice lighter. Breezier. Because he had to be joking. Didn't he? "You should know, that makes me want to take out a subscription to a tacky tabloid newspaper immediately. In your name."

"That friend of yours," he muttered, which didn't make any sense until Cleo saw the way he was looking at her, with that considering gleam in his gaze, as though he was puzzling her out. As though she was a puzzle herself. "The lawyer in New York."

She opened her mouth to correct him, to remind him that Jessie lived in New Orleans, halfway across the country from New York—but didn't.

"Don't waste your time reading the papers, Cleo," he said shortly. An order, not a request. "They're not worth the paper they're printed on and that goes double for the online versions."

"I considered your advice then and now," she told him after a moment, and her tone wasn't light at all, that flare of temper inside her far more like a bonfire, and she was sure he could see it in the way she glared at him. "I believe I'll have to reject it. But thank you."

She regretted it when he rolled away from her, coming up to sit on the edge of her bed. He raked his hands through that thick, coffee-black hair that she loved to run through her own fingers, but he kept his back to her.

"It is of no matter," he said, and she was glad she

couldn't see his face then. "You will be pregnant soon enough and the world can occupy itself with counting to nine months however it thinks best. No matter what you read."

Cleo felt cold, though she couldn't possibly be cold when she'd been overheated five seconds ago, and she pulled the flung-aside sheet over her as if she thought she might get a chill in the perfectly warm room.

"I'm not planning to get pregnant anytime soon, Khaled." She didn't know why her voice was so careful, as if there were imminent danger here. As if there were traps laid all over the floor, the bed, and the slightest sound might trigger them.

"Aren't you?"

"Of course not." She wished he would look at her, and then he did and she wished he'd spare her all that darkness and brooding power that made her shiver deep inside. "I'm only twenty-five."

"You are a woman full grown," he replied after a moment, that hard face unreadable. "And I require heirs." A beat, as if he heard how clinical and medieval that sounded, how it ricocheted between them like a bullet. "I want children, Cleo. *Our* children."

"But…" Cleo couldn't understand why her chest felt so tight. When this was only logical, wasn't it? That he should ask… But then, he wasn't asking. "You don't mean now?"

"Why not now?" Yet the smile he aimed at her didn't quite meet his eyes, and she pulled the sheet tighter to her.

Relax, she told herself. *He can't* order *you pregnant!*

"This is probably something we should have talked about before we got married. Like so many other things, like sleeping arrangements and *schedules.*" She swallowed, eyeing him. "I don't think straight when you touch me, I guess."

His hard mouth softened a shade. "Nor do I."

He sounded significantly more baleful than she had, but she was encouraged anyway.

"The good news," she said calmly, a great deal more calmly than she actually felt, "is that we can take our time making this kind of decision."

"Cleo." He moved then, and while there was a ruthlessness in the way he came across the wide mattress until he leaned over her, she got caught in the poetry of it. The sheer athletic perfection of this man, the way she always did. The way she thought she always would, and for the first time, that inevitability felt hollow. "We haven't taken any precautions. Ever. I assumed we were both on the same page. But let's be clear. Do you want children? My children?"

"Yes." But she couldn't really imagine it, and she couldn't have said why. "But not—"

Not now, she wanted to say, but couldn't.

Not when he was so fierce, so close, so dangerous and compelling at once, and she thought she might die if he looked at her in disappointment. With pity. With the knowledge that she was as plain and pointless and frigid as Brian had decided she was. As she was still so afraid Khaled would realize she was, after all.

"That's agreement enough," he murmured when she didn't continue.

He angled himself closer, and she had the barest shred of a moment to wonder if he did that deliberately, if he used that fire between them—

But no. That was crazy.

"A meeting of the minds, is it not?" he asked.

And he took her mouth again with all that consummate skill, that wondrous fire, and Cleo didn't have the chance to tell him that she was still using the year's worth of birth control pills she'd brought with her on her back-packing trip.

Not then and not later, when he smiled down at her in that way that she knew meant he believed the matter was settled. Solved.

She didn't tell him that she hadn't stopped taking those pills in these past months. That she'd taken one every morning when she brushed her teeth the way she always had at home, even during their week in the oasis. That it was one of the only routines she'd kept from her old life.

She would tell him when they discussed this further, she assured herself. She wasn't trying to deceive him, she was waiting to get to know him better. He would understand that. Cleo was sure he would.

Which was why she also didn't tell him that she had no intention of stopping them.

"Have you tired so quickly of the marital bed?"

Khaled glared at the shadow that detached itself from the wall outside Cleo's rooms so much later that night that it was well into morning and became Nasser.

"You are the only man alive who would dare to say such a thing to my face," he said in a low voice. "And the only man I will not kill for such temerity."

Nasser smiled, unperturbed. "And well do I know it."

Khaled started walking, smoothing an unnecessary hand over his shirt as he moved down the long hall that led toward his office. Always his office. Always something else to be done. Always another fire to put out.

And never the fire he craved most.

"My duties did not suddenly come to an end with a great feast and a brand-new wife," he said darkly. "I must secure the future of Jhurat. You know this as well as I do. And there is one very easy way to do that."

"Ah." His old friend was quiet for a moment. Then,

"Babies. That would cement your line as Talaat has not, and secure your position in the eyes of the world nicely, wouldn't it? Everyone loves a happy family."

"Fairy tales for all." He hardly recognized his own voice.

Yet not for him. Never for him.

That week at the oasis, ripe with longing and yearning and shot through with glimpses of the man he'd never be, the life he'd never lead, had been a mistake.

"A man who must do for duty what he would do anyway for love should look happier, Your Excellency," Nasser murmured after a moment, when there was nothing in the grand hallway but the sound of their feet against the polished marble floor, bouncing back at them from the ornamental columns. "Should he not?"

"This isn't about happiness," Khaled bit out, and he understood that he shouldn't be so angry. That there was no need for this intensity. Worse, that Nasser saw all the things he didn't wish to admit to himself. But he couldn't seem to stop. "Or love, God forbid. This is about Jhurat."

"Of course," Nasser said in his soft way, which meant he didn't wish to argue further, not that he agreed.

Later, Khaled sat at the ostentatious desk that his grandfather had claimed as a spoil of an old war and listened with only half his attention to the conference call with his ministers, most of them handpicked by his father and bristling with their own mortality. Their job was to be fatalistic, he knew, and they rose to the challenge this morning the way they always did.

Talaat's rebels were taking over the country while they did nothing! Talaat would foment civil war if they weren't vigilant! Talaat would topple the government with a single meeting of his agitators in this or that village square—had already done so, if the reports were true!

Khaled didn't believe the situation was quite as dire as

it seemed in the dark and ever-gloomy imaginings of old men, he was tired unto his own death of that pain in his ass, Talaat, and anyway, he could see only Cleo.

His brown mouse of a wife, whom he hadn't been able to banish from his thoughts as he'd planned, and whom he hadn't thought of as a *mouse* in a disturbingly long while. If ever. His wife, who consumed him still and always, like an addiction. He didn't understand it. Every night he promised himself he would break the cycle, and every night he betrayed himself and went to her anyway.

Khaled couldn't seem to get enough of her.

She haunted him, and he hated it. Their week in the oasis had been meant to break this unreasonable hold she had on him—this *need* for her that was only getting worse. That roared into something darker and wilder when she stood up to him, almost as if he wanted her defiance, her strength, as much as he wanted her. As if it called to that part of him he'd been denying for so long it was second nature to him now.

The man, not the sultan.

When of course he didn't want that. He wanted a meek, biddable, obedient wife—the one he'd thought she was when he'd found her. Khaled shoved aside the small voice inside that whispered that he hadn't found her to be anything of the sort. That he'd only taken her back to the palace in the first place because she'd refused to back down....

He had it all planned. Cleo would bear his heirs and take them to the summer palace near the sea as his own mother had done with him and Amira, where the air was better and the climate milder. Where they would grow up as unfettered as possible. Far away from here.

Leaving him free to lose himself in the endless siege of his responsibilities the way he always had before. The way his father and grandfather had done before him. The way he needed to do again, Khaled knew, lest he lose what he'd spent his entire adult life fighting for.

He wondered then, sitting back in his chair and making assenting noises into the phone even though he hardly knew what was under discussion, what it would be like if he stopped. Stopped trying to cage her, to keep her within the distinct lines he'd drawn for her. Stopped fighting himself and the man in him who wanted what he wanted. What if he indulged her—and himself in the process? Stopped trying to keep her as far away from him as he could?

He thought of that challenging light in her pretty gaze tonight when she'd told him she wanted to take out a subscription to a tabloid paper. In his name, no less. He thought of that frown of hers that had told him from the start she saw the man before the sultan, that she wasn't blindly in awe of him like everyone else.

But this country was his life. It had ruined his father and it would ruin him, too, in his time. Just as it had destroyed his mother when he'd been twenty. He'd spent most of his life watching his mother fight for his father's attention, so deliriously happy when she'd received it and then so destroyed when it was gone again. She'd retreated from life a long time before she had simply stopped fighting for the scraps of his father's attention. Had it been disease that had taken her or her own broken heart?

And meanwhile, his father had tried to please both his woman and his people and had failed them both.

Jhurat had been exacting a terrible tithe from his family for five generations, one after the next down through the ages, and he didn't imagine that would ever end. And despite everything, he loved this place as he loved his own blood. His own bones. Every time-worn rock that made it what it was, every sun-beaten border so many of his ancestors had bled over, every grain of sand in the great desert and the thick oil beneath.

It was who he was. It was all he was.

There was no space inside him for a woman with eyes as sweet as honey and a smile like the sun when there was Jhurat, its deserts and whitewashed cities, its citadels and spires, like scars carved directly on his heart. There was no room for this dangerous longing that kicked at him even now, when he'd spent another long night indulging himself in her delectable heat and should have been sated. When he should have forgotten her the moment he'd left that bedroom.

When he shouldn't have gone to her in the first place.

Khaled couldn't understand why he had. Why he always did. Why he no doubt would again, tonight and every night, like an obsessed, lovesick fool.

Cleo was a means to an end, nothing more. And she needed to get pregnant, and soon, so he could put some space between them. So he could stop going to her night after night and feeling these things he couldn't allow himself to feel. So he could stop this madness, this lust, this *need*.

Because Khaled had never had the option to be that man only she seemed to call out in him. He never would.

"And how is life with my darling brother?" Amira asked at breakfast one morning, making no attempt to keep the lash from her voice.

She was home for her long winter break from her boarding school and Cleo didn't want to admit how nice it was to eat with something other than her own thoughts. Even if that something was a snide teenager.

Not that she knew how to answer the question. It had been a few months since she'd lied by omission about her birth control pills, and nothing had changed. She saw Khaled even less by day, but he was far more intense when he appeared in her bedroom at night. More demanding. More powerfully raw.

And she'd become an expert at ignoring all the rest of the dark things she didn't want to admit were there, simmering away beneath the surface of her pretty, perfect life. Her happily ever after in action.

"Wonderful," she said, smiling benevolently at her sister-in-law, and possibly much too widely. She remembered that Khaled had once suggested that Amira needed feminine guidance, and tried to look like someone who might offer such a thing. "Everything is absolutely wonderful."

Amira sniffed. "That doesn't sound much like the Khaled I know."

"Why don't you tell me about that Khaled, then?" Cleo asked brightly. She assured herself that she was simply diverting her sister-in-law's teenage spleen, not pathetically digging for scraps of information on a man she barely knew, yet happened to be married to anyway.

"Khaled is the sultan," Amira said bitterly. "The end."

"You understand that he has a tremendous amount of responsibility—"

Amira blew out an aggrieved sigh, cutting Cleo off.

"I understand that he will do anything for Jhurat. Do you think he would have married you if he didn't get something from it? That's the way he is. If you cease to be of use, you cease to exist. Trust me, Cleo. I know."

"There is more to life than responsibility," Cleo said gently. "Even for a sultan."

Her sister-in-law looked scornful for a moment—then her expression shifted into something Cleo was terrified to identify, it looked so much like pity.

"Not for Khaled," she said, and her voice was almost kind. "He *is* Jhurat, and it will kill him, the same way it killed our mother. It took our father's mind, turned cousin against cousin and caused our family endless misery. He is cursed. You should know that better than anyone, Cleo."

"Maybe you don't know your brother as well as you think," Cleo said staunchly, but her fingers gripped her fork too tightly, and her eggs had gone cold.

"And maybe you don't know him at all," Amira replied, and the worst part was, there wasn't a trace of her usual biting tone when she said it.

CHAPTER SIX

SEVERAL EVENINGS LATER, Cleo finally had a night to herself. She left the judgmental Margery behind down in the office, made her serene way up to her suite and then locked herself away in the luxurious and sprawling rooms that were her only private space. There was no one to watch her smile and comment on its brightness here, or compare it to last week's smiles and decide that any deviation meant she was carrying twins.

Cleo didn't feel much like smiling when she was finally alone. Even so, she refused to succumb to that rolling, twisting, terrible thing inside her, black like ink and covered in spikes. She wouldn't listen to those voices in her head whispering that *of course* Amira had been right at breakfast the other day. That everyone had been right.

That deny it all she might, she'd made a terrible mistake.

You will not cry, she ordered herself harshly.

Cleo stripped herself of her latest breathlessly chic clothes—all of which Margery had chosen and Karima had laid out for her without any input from Cleo—and pulled on the silk wrapper that she now wore in place of any comfortable lounging clothes. It took her a few moments and the use of a heavy footstool she had to drag in from the bedroom, but she managed to climb up to the farthest shelf in the large and airy adjoining room that was her closet and pull down her battered backpack from its hiding place.

She let that black, spiked thing crash through her then, as she held the beat-up old pack to her like a security blanket. The sudden, deep heaviness almost knocked her from her feet, so hard and fast did it drop through her.

But she was fiercely happy that she'd insisted Karima pack the bag away instead of getting rid of it altogether. She unzipped it now, pretending she didn't notice how her heart was pounding, and smiled at all the too-familiar things packed inside. All her travel clothes. The clothes she'd bought while she was in the U.K., gradually phasing out all the things that reminded her of home and Brian and that whole part of her life and replacing them with things that had made her feel intrepid and brave. Like the world traveler she'd wanted to be, sophisticated and jaded and unlikely to be fooled by anyone ever again.

The clothes she hadn't worn since she'd come to Jhurat. When she'd traded one adventure for another, one identity for the next, with a whole new wardrobe to go with it.

As though she was nothing but a chameleon. Like none of this was real—it was merely one more change of clothes.

Cleo slung the pack into a corner even though she knew she'd have to put it back where she'd found it if she didn't want Karima to notice what she'd been up to, but frowned when it *thunked* against the wall. She went over and crouched down, rifling through the pockets until she found what had made the noise.

It was a mobile phone and a charger. Neither hers.

She stared at both for a long time. And then she went back into the bedroom and fired up her laptop. It was only when she clicked on the Skype icon on her computer screen that it occurred to her how long it had been since she'd done it last. So long that she hesitated before she clicked on Jessie's name—

But she did it anyway. And Jessie answered at once, despite the fact that it was mid-morning in New Orleans and she was at work. That heavy thing inside of Cleo shifted in a drunken sort of tilt that made her stomach flip over, and it was hard to look at her oldest friend suddenly. At those warm brown eyes that saw too much, the strawberry-blond hair that had always been in complete disarray throughout their youth that Jessie wore in a sleek style befitting the high-powered attorney she was now, or the faint crease of concern in her friend's brow.

"I found the phone," Cleo said, as much to start the conversation as to skip over the uncomfortable things she didn't want to address, such as why she'd been out of touch for months despite all the emails Jessie had sent with those articles Cleo wasn't supposed to read. "A wedding gift, I'm guessing?"

"Are you mad at me?" Jessie leaned closer to her screen, a world away and yet it felt like she was *right there* with Cleo—and Cleo wanted that so much it made her eyes glaze over with emotion. "It was my attempt to re-create our youth."

"Did we have secret phones? I remember sneaking out to see that embarrassing concert and that boy you liked, but no secret phones."

"We had *pretend* secret phones," Jessie said, and sighed as if she couldn't believe Cleo didn't remember that. "That made them *particularly* secret."

"Do you have a secret phone now, too?" Cleo asked. "Or is it only for me?"

She'd meant that to come out light and easy, but it didn't, and she felt a lump in her throat as Jessie studied her face through the screen.

"I always like to have an escape hatch, Cleo," she said softly, after a long moment. "You know that."

"That's the lawyer in you, I guess."

"No, that's what happens when you grow up with four brothers, all of whom think it's hilarious to lock you in your room whenever they think you're being annoying." Jessie sat back in her seat and smiled brightly, and Cleo thought she'd never loved her more. "How's my favorite newlywed?"

And Cleo could have told her. Jessie was the only one she'd have considered telling, in fact, and who cared that it was all so twisted and tangled inside of her—but she opened her mouth and found she couldn't do it.

Because the things she felt for Khaled consumed her whole. Made her feel that there was something wrong with her that she could feel *so much*. That was the truth no matter how she fought against it.

She might not know him, but she was pretty sure she loved him.

Cleo had thought she loved Brian, and what she'd felt for him even in their happy beginning had been pale and silly compared to this. She wondered if he'd known that. If that had been why he'd done what he did. And how could she hold on to all that bitterness she'd been carrying around when the truth was, if Brian hadn't cheated on her, Cleo would never be here? She'd never have met Khaled.

And she couldn't imagine that. She might not be as happy in her fantasy life as she'd assumed she would be, but she couldn't imagine not being in it.

"Sometimes it's hard to separate the sultan from the man," she admitted to Jessie in a rushed sort of whisper, and even that felt like a betrayal.

Jessie met her gaze, her brown eyes uncompromising, as if she knew every last thing Cleo wasn't saying.

"Listen to me." Jessie used her lawyer voice. "You're the most fearless person I know. You didn't accept what Brian did to you the way a lot of people would have, especially so close to the wedding. You walked away and wandered the world by yourself. You married a terrifying man who might as well be a freaking king. There isn't a single thing you can't do if you put your mind to it."

"You're right," Cleo said, as though it came from somewhere deep in her gut. "I did."

That was why, when she and Jessie had finished catching up and vowing to stay in better touch this time, when she'd had her dinner on a tray again, she decided she was going to do something about all of this. Because she'd grown too quiet since the oasis. She'd become too worried about being the perfect sultan's wife when what she should have been worrying about was how to be herself.

She needed to make her life, her man, her marriage, *hers*. Because she refused to accept that this was a mistake. Amira and Margery and her sisters—they didn't know the truth of things between Cleo and Khaled. She could have married Brian. Everyone had urged her to forgive him, and the wedding had already been planned and paid for. It would have been the easiest thing in the world to simply surrender herself to his promises and apologies, but she hadn't done it.

She'd wanted more. She'd wanted *better*. She'd wanted the damned fairy tale everyone told her didn't exist, and she'd found it. She'd found Khaled.

She could fight for him, too.

Cleo waited until it was late. She sneaked down the back hall over to the sultan's private wing of the palace, then in through the antechamber where—she'd learned in her history lessons—ancient Jhuratan sultans had held court with their most trusted advisers beneath the frescoed ceilings. It was more beautiful than she'd anticipated, more hauntingly evocative than the photographs and more intimidating, too. But she forced herself forward despite the trickle of unease that moved in her. She cracked open the towering door that led to Khaled's bedroom and crept inside.

Walked inside, she corrected herself, and lifted her head up high while she did it.

She had every right to be here. This was her marriage, too.

The room looked exactly like a sultan's inner sanctum should, she thought, pausing to take in the glory of the bedchamber as it soared all around her. It was vast and lush as befitted a desert ruler with an ancient title. Dark crimsons and black woods, heavily masculine furniture and ornate details clearly dating back centuries, all competing and dominating and somehow working together with a monolithic bed that looked more like an imposing stage set high up on a raised dais.

That was where she waited for her husband. Because she was fearless and intrepid, damn it, and this was her happy ever after.

But she was naked when she slipped between his whisper-soft sheets. Just to make sure.

"What are you doing here?"

Khaled's voice was low, but the dark thunder in it jolted Cleo awake.

For a moment she didn't know where she was, and then it came back to her: she was in Khaled's bedroom. In his bed.

And, she remembered as she shifted and the silken sheets caressed her, she was naked.

"I didn't mean to fall asleep," she told him, and that was when the way he was standing there at the foot of the bed, watching her with an alarming stillness, registered. Her heart gave a great kick.

He looked dangerous and impossibly remote at once, and that was only the way his too-gray eyes glittered in the soft light.

Khaled was dressed in clothes she'd never seen him

wear before—a dark black T-shirt that clung to his muscular shoulders and a pair of exercise trousers that made his legs look even more powerful—with his arms crossed over his flat chest. And he was scowling at her, every inch of him the sultan she'd seen first on that street, mighty and powerful and great beyond measure. Her throat went dry.

"You go to the gym?" It was the first thing she could think of, and it was better than addressing the gnawing thing that made her feel scooped hollow behind her breastbone. "I guess that explains…" She shifted to sitting position, letting the sheets fall away, but he didn't react the way she'd expected he would. She nodded in his direction, at all that hard-packed, lean muscle, from his shoulders to that ridged wonder of an abdomen. *"…that."*

"Cleo."

She didn't like the clipped way he said that, to say nothing of the dark way he was looking at her, as if she had trespassed. As if she'd ruined something by her presence here—but no. She couldn't let herself think like that.

"I will ask you again. Why are you here?"

"Khaled."

She tried to make her own voice soft. Encouraging. *Inviting.* She arched her back slightly and presented herself to him the way she knew he liked, the way that often made him growl deep in his throat like some kind of panther. She wanted that. She wanted *him*.

"I'm your wife. I'm in your bed. Why do you think I'm here?"

His gaze moved from hers to trace over her, making her nipples prickle in instant awareness, making her stomach pull taut, making her feel almost proud of the wild heat that sparked in the air between them. Uncontrollable. Unmistakable. Making her wish she had the nerve to simply crawl toward him and take what she wanted, what she knew he wanted, because this was where they came together best. This fire. This sweet, intoxicating burn. This was their communion. She thought she understood it now.

"If I wanted you," he said, very distinctly, very coldly, "I would have come for you."

It took her a moment to process that. One beat of her heart, then another—and that second one so hard it was jarring. It made her stomach drop. It made her go numb, then cold.

"What?"

"I see I didn't make myself clear." His tone was off-hand, almost bored, but there was a storm in his gray eyes. A deep blackness, thick and harsh, as if he were tortured. She could see it. It pressed at her on all sides. "I don't find this kind of thing appealing."

Nothing he was saying made any sense. Cleo could only stare at him, frozen solid—and she remembered this feeling. She'd experienced it once before, when she'd used her key in Brian's front door and walked inside, then stood there in the living room doorway, trying to make sense of what was happening right there on the floor in front of her.

This was worse.

"I've tried to make allowances for the differences in our ages. Our cultures." Khaled's voice was a terrible glide of sound, dark and cutting and still so smooth as it tore into her, ripping her into ragged little strips, one after the next. "The disparity in our breeding. But I'm afraid this is unacceptable."

He sounded the way he had that first evening, out in the street, when he'd talked of detainment and kidnapping—except this time, she could see something bright and harsh behind his fierce expression, as if this was hurting him. Killing him.

As if he couldn't stop.

But then what he'd said echoed inside of her, like the vicious backhanded slap it was. Cleo flushed, hot and awful.

And then her temper swept in behind it, burning through her, and that, at least, felt like a reprieve.

"What did you just say to me?" she demanded.

"I am talking about *this*." He nodded toward her, his eyes glittering hot though he didn't move from where he stood in terrible judgment at the foot of the bed, not so much as an inch, as if he'd been hewn from granite. "I am talking about this display of yours."

And then, finally, he looked at her the way she'd always known he would. The way she'd been expecting he would from the start. With nothing but pity.

"Perhaps it is common in Ohio to indulge in such vulgarity," he said coolly, "but this is Jhurat and I expect far better from my wife."

Cleo waited to feel decimated. Wiped out. Destroyed. But the only thing that hummed in her was temper, huge and encompassing, and she squared her shoulders as though she was warding off a blow.

"I expect better from you, Khaled. Much better."

He blinked. "I beg your pardon?" Each word was black ice. Treacherous and frozen. "I am the Sultan of Jhurat. There is no better."

"I thought you were a good man. An honorable one."

He went so still it was as though he'd become the statue of himself that would one day grace some corner or another of the palace, and the tension in the room stretched so thin Cleo thought it might break her in half. She knelt there before him like the meek offering she suspected he wanted and she wondered, sickened, what she'd become without realizing it while she'd been chasing down fairy tales. But what truly galled her was that what bothered her most was that he was so upset. That he was so obviously *hurt*.

She had to fight against that trembling deep inside her that she didn't want him to see. She had to struggle not to weep. And she wanted—suddenly and completely—to run away again, to leave Khaled behind like one more demon and find herself a different life somewhere new.

But she'd already done that, hadn't she? And this certainly didn't feel as if the geographic cure was working.

"Tell me what this is," he urged her after a moment so long she'd thought he really had turned to stone. "I feel certain I've made clear to you what I think of disrespect."

"Then respect *me,*" she blurted out, then wished at once she hadn't, because he braced himself as if he was about to strike—

And then he did.

"Respect what?" he asked, almost conversationally, his gaze implacable and cruel as it bored into her. "The creature who stumbled across my sister on a city street, who would never have attracted my notice otherwise? Or the elegant bride I created out of the barest of raw materials to suit my purposes? Which of those are you, Cleo? Which version do you imagine I should respect?"

"Stop it." It hurt to speak. To breathe. "I'm your *wife.*"

"You seem to be laboring under some misconceptions concerning that role." He was still speaking in that calm, viciously casual tone with the jagged edge beneath it, aware—she could tell from that broken thing in his gaze that looked like suffering but couldn't be—that every word was pummeling her. That every word was cracking her apart, tearing strips from her, and he had no intention of stopping it. That he wanted this, no matter how badly it hurt her. Or him. "You are a pawn."

"Khaled—"

"My country kept the outside world at bay for so long that we came to be seen as nothing but barbarians. It is my job—my sworn duty—to change that perception and our fortunes along with it, but how? And then you stumbled into my life. The standard-issue American nobody."

She thought she said his name again, but her throat was too tight, she felt too raw and she understood she didn't make a sound. And that on some level, she'd been waiting for him to say something like this since he'd poured her tea.

His cruel mouth looked surprisingly vulnerable for a moment, his gray gaze stark and hollow, but then it was gone. Cleo knew she must have imagined it.

"There isn't a single thing about you that is anything but ordinary, Cleo, and that is precisely why I wanted you. It is the only reason I wanted you. I spun you into a princess from a handful of straw."

She thought she was numb—but surely it would hurt less if she was? He leaned closer, his gray gaze nearly silver with temper and that dark thing beneath it that made her stomach knot. And Cleo had always been a fighter. She had always stood up for herself, eventually. How many times had she proved that? And yet here, tonight, when it would never matter more, she couldn't seem to do anything but wait for the next blow.

"And look how beautifully you have served your purpose," Khaled continued, cruel and remote, like the god she'd imagined him so many times before but this time, he was anything but benevolent. "But I cannot have you getting ideas above your station. You are my wife, yes, but the only thing that means to me is that sooner or later, you will provide me with children."

"To do what?" she heard herself say in an awful voice, thick with all the things she couldn't seem to say, couldn't let herself feel for fear it would destroy her even more than he already had, couldn't even process while she still sat there before him and was skewered. Over and over again. "Obey more of your commands? So you can have a whole collection of helpless, servile creatures to do your bidding?"

He smiled, and it sliced through her. "If you do not obey me, Cleo, I will simply replace you."

She didn't know what it said about her that even now, even after what had transpired between them this night, she couldn't believe he'd said that. That she could feel still more pain. That she could feel shattered all over again.

"Khaled." Where did that voice come from? So quiet and broken, but still hers—as if it was pushed out from the very heart of her. She lifted her hands up and held them out in supplication, and she couldn't even hate herself for it. She understood, somehow, that it was strength, not surrender. "This is getting out of control. I don't want to challenge you. I only want to *be* with you. I want a partner, a true marriage—"

"I don't."

Stark and flat. Matter-of-fact.

The end, that voice within her stated.

Cleo's mouth dropped open, and it was only when she shut it with an audible snap and happened to look down that she realized she was clenching her hands so hard she'd broken the skin on her own palms with her fingernails.

"But…"

She didn't know why she was still talking. As if he hadn't laid her out flat, and if the expression on his face was anything to go by, deliberately. As if there was anything left to talk about with a man who thought so little of her.

Then again, there was one thing. One truth, however tiny it seemed here. One small point of light that somehow, she wanted to believe was worth the darkness.

She swallowed, and then she said it. "I love you."

It went through him like electricity—a long charge, harsh and bright. Khaled stiffened, those three words pounding into him like enemy gunfire, lighting him up.

Filling him with fury and grief.

You have no choice, he reminded himself, and her words proved it. They were exactly what he'd wanted to avoid. They were her future disaster in the making, her own ruin lying there before him, as naked and as vulnerable as she was.

He wished he was another man. He wished he was anyone but who he was, chained to this palace, this country, this life he'd never chosen.

"It has only been a little while," he told her, the bastard that he was, determined to stop her from going any further down this road. Saving her from her own doom, though the betrayed look on her lovely face, in her honey-colored eyes, told him she wouldn't see it that way. "You will no doubt fall out of love as quickly."

And then he moved the way he'd wanted to the moment he'd realized what that unusual shape was in the center of his bed. The moment he'd understood it was Cleo, his Cleo, her hair spread out around her and those marvelously responsive breasts bared to his view, arrayed before him like the perfect sacrifice to his own eternal need for her.

He wanted her. More than he wanted his next breath. And he couldn't have that, so he had to do whatever he could to make her hate him. It was better that way. It was far safer for her, no matter how it felt to her—to him— now. It was his gift to her.

He should have given it to her far sooner, he knew.

Khaled came up and onto the bed until he was right there before her, too fast for her to do anything but watch him with that same stunned look on her face, as the latest horrible thing he'd thrown at her reverberated in the air between them. She pulled back, belatedly, and he simply took her chin in his hand to make her look at him.

She shuddered, but she didn't knock his fingers away. She didn't even try.

If you won't protect yourself, he thought bitterly, that howling thing inside him gathering force and speed, punching out pieces of him as it went, *then I must.*

"What you love is sex," he grated at her, and he saw it land. Hard. "You love what I can do to you with the faintest touch. No matter what I say to you or what I do, you still come when I command it."

"No." But it was only a whisper, and her eyes were dark and huge.

"You crave my touch," he said in that same dark way, so low it was almost as if he was talking to himself. He wished he was. "Like there is nothing else on this earth that matters."

And he proved it, reaching over with his other hand and cupping her breast, watching the way her nipple hardened at once. Watching the red flush high on her cheeks that he knew by now meant she melted for him below. Showing her all the ways she wanted him, even now.

"I love *you*," she said again, and more fiercely.

But then, she didn't know that he'd been broken long before he'd met her, and had accepted it. Embraced it. That he'd never imagined there would be any light at all in this dark and dutiful life of his. That he'd had no idea she would burn this bright, tempting him to ignore his blood, his duty, his country, the price he knew they'd both have to pay—anything to have her. Anything.

It would kill him. He was certain of it.

"Cleo, please." His words were hard, his voice far colder than he felt. "You hardly know me. You're an inexperienced woman who clearly hasn't had anything like decent sex before. I don't *want* you to know me. I don't want you to do anything but what you're told."

"But I can't—"

"You can."

And then he kissed her like a starving man, with all the

agony he couldn't show her, all the things he wanted that he knew he couldn't have. Love. A true marriage. *Her.* He kissed her as though he thought might never kiss her again.

That fire that always roared between them was much brighter tonight. Wilder. Or she was, burning as hot and as golden and as out of his reach as the moon.

Khaled took her over, kissing her again and again until she wrapped her arms around him and kissed him back. Then he simply bore her back to the bed, settling himself between her thighs, hard where she was soft, and there was no pretending they weren't both as desperate as they'd ever been.

Nasser had warned him long ago that he would break her heart. He should have listened. He should have understood that in the end, if he wanted to protect this surprising woman who had lodged herself so unexpectedly inside his own chest, it would be his heart that shattered.

Especially when he saw her tears.

"Don't," he whispered, the sound very nearly broken, as if he could command her not to cry.

"Is that an order, Your Excellency?" she asked, bitterly, and when he kissed her again she tasted of salt and heat, and there was that hollow thing in him, loud and devastating.

"Cleo—" he began, and he didn't know what he might have said.

But she didn't let him continue. She wound her arms around his neck and her legs around his hips and he let her pull him down against her. So they could burn in this madness together. So they could forget.

So he could save her instead of himself.

He rocked his hips against hers, making her shudder in that instant, ecstatic response he couldn't get enough of. He bent to her breasts and lavished them with his mouth, his hands, even his teeth. She writhed beneath him, arching toward his mouth, her cries growing more desperate the closer she came—

She groaned when he lifted his head. And her gaze was a dark storm of gold when she looked up at him, watching as he reached down between them to free himself from his exercise trousers.

Khaled thought he might die if he didn't get inside her, now. He thought he might die anyway and somehow, tonight, he didn't much care.

"And where does this fall within your chilly little concept of marriage?" she bit out, and he could see everything right there in her gaze, as open and as perfect as she was. The love he'd thrown back in her face, her deep hurt, and her own unmistakable need. Everything. "Or are you going to pretend this is nothing but procreation?"

He slicked himself through her heat and watched the burn of it shiver through her, fighting back his own shudder as the flames that licked between them stretched bright and high.

"Behave," he gritted at her as if he was in control of this, of her, of his own wild response, "and this will be your reward. Disobey me, and this will be nothing but a memory."

He toyed with her then, holding himself still at her entrance and ignoring her attempts to twist her hips, to take him inside her. Ignoring the nails she dug into his shoulders, the desperate way she groaned out his name.

Ignoring everything but her inevitable surrender.

Because there was no other way. No other choice. There never had been.

"I hate you," she moaned at him, and it shouldn't have hurt.

It was what he wanted. It was why he'd done this tonight, instead of following the more animal urge he'd had when he'd found her here. This was the easiest way to save her, and he knew it.

"Hate me if you must," he urged her, hoarse and dark, and then he thrust into her with a hard, sure stroke that made her moan. He pulled her closer so his mouth was at her ear, and then he began to move, delighting in each and every exquisite sound she made, helpless and wild and his, even now. "I don't care. But you will obey."

And she did.

Again and again, until the light began to creep in through his windows. Until she was ruined and lost and completely destroyed. Until he seemed satisfied enough that she'd received his brutal message that he finally passed out beside her the way he hadn't done since their time in the oasis.

Cleo didn't sleep. She couldn't. She lay by his side, beneath one heavy arm, pulled close up against him as if they fit.

She was wrung out. Her body still thrummed with everything they'd done, all the ways he'd taken her, all the things he'd done to demonstrate his power over her no matter what terrible things he said. She'd loved them all, and she hated herself for it.

And she knew one thing with perfect, resounding clarity: she couldn't do this any longer. It was one thing to lose herself the way she'd done in all these strange months since he'd plucked her from the street. She couldn't imagine how she'd ever forgive herself for pursuing that fantasy of hers so single-mindedly she'd lost sight of reality, but at least it was only her in this. She'd chosen him.

But how could she possibly bring a child into this mess the way he seemed so determined to do? What would she teach a baby—that it was acceptable to live like this, so deeply controlled? Broken into pieces and ignored unless called for?

Khaled was like a drug. She wanted him, even now. Her

heart ached for him, as if it didn't care that he was the one who'd hammered it to pieces in the first place.

And she finally understood what she should have known from the start, what so many people had tried to tell her: that she couldn't stay here. That this had been a terrible mistake.

She couldn't do this. She had to go.

Before he figured out why she wasn't getting pregnant the way he wanted. Before all of this got worse. Before she was trapped so securely and so completely in this web of his—sex and command and her broken little heart that wanted so desperately to find the good in him, any good in him, that believed in that fairy tale she'd spun around this empty life they led—that she forgot she'd ever been anything but his.

His possession. His pawn. Whatever he made her. Whatever he desired.

She had to leave him.

While she still could.

CHAPTER SEVEN

"YOUR WIFE IS ENCHANTING!" the Italian businessman cried, much too enthusiastically for Khaled's liking, especially when he had his equally enthusiastic hands on Cleo while he was saying it.

But Khaled smiled because it was the expected thing and they were in the full glare of a very public gala, and restrained himself from knocking the man's bristly mustache away from Cleo's outstretched hands. Barely.

Mine, he thought, the way he always did, because even dressed in formal clothes and smiling politely for the cameras, Khaled was little more than a caveman where this woman was concerned. *His* woman.

It was the height of winter in Vienna and he was already weary of this nonsense. They'd been traveling for several weeks now, hitting one event after another across Europe so that Khaled could court captains of industry like the one currently slobbering over his wife. He was tired.

He was tired of touting his vision of a new Jhurat like a snake-oil salesman. He was tired of explaining all the reasons this or that industry should plant new roots in Jhuratan soil. He was tired of dancing and smiling and acting like one among the many over-titled idiots who cluttered up the European ballrooms, none of them with the slightest idea of what it meant to truly fight for anything.

And he was tired, so very tired, of the icy cold perfection of his wife.

He had to hand it to her, Khaled thought darkly as he watched her latest performance—making the besotted Italian man lapse into what sounded like poetry while never forgetting the equally smitten Swiss banker on her left. Cleo learned her lessons quickly. Especially the ones he'd taught her.

She was perfect tonight. She'd been perfect for weeks, come to that. She oozed aristocratic grace from every pore, a feat indeed, given that everyone who saw her knew who she was and that she hadn't a drop of blue blood in her. Since that awful night in his bedchamber, she hadn't so much as lifted a single silken brow against him. No hint of her charming defiance, no trace of that glorious smile of hers, no more attempts on her part to make him laugh. She'd woken up that following morning and she'd simply been…perfect.

Tonight she was holding court with an ease that suggested she'd spent her whole life preparing for this role, which Khaled had to remind himself was an illusion. She was a vision in a column of shimmering silver that both flattered her figure and preserved her modesty at once, as befitted a woman who served as an advertisement for a conservative country.

She seemed as at ease in her fashionably high heels as she was to find herself surrounded by a pack of international philanthropists known as much for their ruthlessness as for their checkbooks. Her lovely hair—all those blondes and caramels and reds Khaled could never get his fill of—was swept back into an elegant twist and anointed with pearls and diamonds on delicate combs, and when he had walked into her dressing room to collect her she'd smiled at him as though he was anyone. Just another potential donor she needed to charm. Anonymous.

She'd been so bright and so beautiful—yet so remote—that he'd had no choice but to drop to his knees right there, pulling that gleaming silver fabric up to bare her soft thighs before he'd buried his face in that wild heat between her legs.

He'd made her sob out his name, her hands fisted against his shoulders. He'd made her break apart and shake, buck and shiver. And when she came back to herself she looked at him with that same damned smile and thanked him.

Like a perfectly polite stranger.

She was a dream come true. She was exactly what he'd told her, so cruelly, he wanted. She was absolutely perfect.

And he hated it. More with every passing day.

"Come," he muttered when the poetic Italian finally took his leave, trailing a thousand *bellissimas* in his wake, and she turned her lovely, always composed, unreadable face to him. "Dance with me."

Cleo smiled prettily—she always smiled so prettily now, she was so damned obedient, and he couldn't stand how off balance that made him feel—and followed him out onto the dance floor. He took her in his arms and she gazed up at him, serene and lovely.

And he wanted to shove himself under her skin. Make her *react*.

He wanted the old Cleo back. *His* Cleo. That overawed girl who had danced with him in Paris so long ago and gazed at him as if he was the sun and she wanted nothing more than to burn alive in him. That astonishingly courageous backpacker who had stood up to him in a street, when she knew exactly who he was. That surprising, life-altering night she'd melted all over him in his own courtyard at so small a touch.

This is how it has to be, he told himself, the way he always did, though it felt emptier than usual tonight. Or he did. *This is safer for her by far.*

Khaled had never felt so hollow in his life.

"You're scowling," Cleo said now, entirely without inflection, because he had told her she was nothing and she'd taken him at his word. This was entirely his doing.

He should have rejoiced at his success. Instead, he felt nothing but grim. As though he'd blacked out his own sun.

"I find my patience for these events grows thinner all the time," he said, prodded by something he didn't understand to confide in her. The further he pushed her away, the further she disappeared behind that smooth mask of hers, the more he wanted her close. He couldn't recall the last time they'd slept apart, and he'd been considering moving her permanently into his suite in the palace. Because he was a despicable man. The truth of that pressed into him, cold and inescapable. "I find it less and less unreasonable that my father locked himself away in Jhurat and closed off all the borders. It would be easier."

Cleo was silent for a moment. She'd become even more slender in the past few months, and his hand spanned her waist in a way he didn't entirely like. But still she moved with that beautiful elegance of hers, her dancing as exquisite as she was, and it wasn't the first time Khaled wished—deeply and wildly—that he was a different man.

Or even that he'd found a better way to keep her at arm's length.

"You are not your father," she said, her tone measured, her golden gaze meeting his only briefly before sliding away in that deferential manner she'd adopted that made him clench his teeth. "You want more for Jhurat than he did."

"That doesn't mean I'll get it. And I could do more harm than good."

Because that was what he did, wasn't it?

"At least you will have tried," she said after a moment, and he wondered if they were thinking of the same night.

The same vicious words he couldn't take back. That he knew he shouldn't *want* to take back. "That has to be better than hiding out and pretending nothing is happening, doesn't it?"

Their gazes tangled then, and Khaled very nearly missed a step.

He didn't know what surged in him then, making him feel broken open and singed black straight through to his core. He didn't know why he could only look down at her, as shaken as he was cursed, and wonder who this smooth, perfect creature was, who spoke so softly and knew him so well and was lost to him forever.

When, of course, he knew. She was what he'd made her with his very own hands. She was what he'd demanded she'd become. She'd opened herself up wide and he'd smashed her flat.

The truth was, he hadn't truly believed she'd obey him. No matter what he'd said. She never had before.

Cleo held his gaze as if she knew exactly what he was thinking, what he was feeling, and he didn't know what might happen if she—

But she was too perfect. Too remote.

She only smiled at him again, and he hated it.

In bed she was still the Cleo he remembered. She was still his. The cooler and more distant she became while she was in public, the wilder and more raw she was in private. Anything but smooth. Anything but polished. He held on to that with more desperation than he cared to examine.

She hadn't claimed to love him again. He'd broken her of that.

"When we return to Jhurat I want you to see the palace physician," he told her abruptly, and she stiffened in his arms so briefly he almost thought he imagined it.

"Am I ill?"

It was an echo of the old Cleo, that soft yet faintly sharp

question, and it went through him like a shot—but when she tilted her head back to look at him, he saw nothing but that blandness he'd come to despise.

"I don't think so," he said. "Though it would explain a great deal. Do you feel ill?"

"Not in the way you mean." She was insolent and it thrilled him—but then she blinked, that mask of perfection obscuring the Cleo he wanted to see. "Though I believe I ate far too much of that Sacher torte."

She had done nothing but pick at the intensely chocolate cake, a Viennese specialty, that had been presented to them earlier. She had marveled over its richness to their hostess but consumed very little of it.

Not that Khaled had taken to monitoring her every movement like an obsessed fool.

"You're still not pregnant." It came out flat. Like an accusation.

Cleo tilted her head back slightly as if that had been a blow to her chin, and Khaled wished he knew the right words to say to make this better. All of this. But he'd been made from blood and sacrifice, desert justice and the stark, uncompromising Jhuratan sun. He could never spout poetry as that Italian had done. He wouldn't know where to start, and even if he did, he thought he'd end up speaking of battles and losses. Duty and demand. Not the things that mattered here. To her.

But the words he needed tangled in his throat, and it seemed he could only scowl at her when it was the last thing he wanted to do.

"Not yet." She eyed him. "Does that require an apology? I thought it took both of us to succeed or fail in getting pregnant, if I'm remembering my high school biology classes correctly."

Did he imagine that edge to her voice then? That odd sheen in her golden gaze? Or was he merely desperate for any sign of a break in that wall—the wall he'd built himself? His hand tightened at her waist, and he knew he didn't imagine her slight, sharp intake of breath.

"Cleo," he began.

"I don't mean to interrupt, of course," she said, very calmly—as if she was as unmoved by him, by this, as he was nearly unmanned by her. "But I believe those hoteliers you wanted to speak with have arrived."

For a beat, Khaled couldn't remember why he'd want to speak to anyone but Cleo. But then he turned to look and reality reasserted itself. He needed these people, these wealthy, pampered people who lived to throw their money around. That's why he was here. Jhurat required as much foreign investment as possible, and Khaled's role was to convince everyone he spoke to that the only thing medieval about his homeland was the architecture.

Not him. No matter how Cleo inspired him to behave.

"We must talk," he told her, in that stilted, caveman way he couldn't seem to stop. Why was it he could control an entire country and not his own wife?

"Of course," Cleo agreed. He thought she'd say anything to push him even further away, and the fact that he should exult in that, that it indicated he'd succeeded with her, was but one more darkness inside of him to match the rest. One among so many. "Whatever you want."

That was the trouble. Khaled knew what he wanted. What he'd wanted from almost the first moment he'd laid eyes on this woman.

And he still couldn't have it.

It didn't matter what he felt. It never had.

In the end, it was simple.

It had taken months of preparation, Jessie's invaluable counsel in figuring out the best way to leave a man who would never permit it should she ask outright, and a willingness to look directly into that man's face and tell a thousand lies of omission that Cleo still found so much harder than she should have—but that night, it was simple.

When they returned to their hotel suite, Khaled simply eyed her in that hungry, imperative way of his that made every nerve ending inside of her dance into awareness, shrugging out of his sleek formal jacket and yanking at his tie without ever breaking her gaze.

And Cleo felt it as if she'd been dropped into a pit of flames, headfirst.

The way she always did. No matter what he said to her. No matter what he did.

No matter what she thought she *ought* to feel.

"Didn't you want to talk about something?" she asked politely, and it was still so hard to keep her voice smooth. It was more difficult than it should have been to gaze straight back at him as if she was unmoved by him, so dark and imperious and still so damned gorgeous.

Nothing had changed, she reminded herself. Not Khaled, certainly, despite the way he watched her sometimes when he thought she wasn't looking. And that meant her resolve couldn't change, either.

Particularly if he wanted to "talk." And then send her to a doctor, who, she felt certain, would be unlikely to uphold any kind of confidentiality about Cleo's birth control choices when it pertained to the sultan's desire for heirs.

"Tomorrow," he muttered, watching her as if she were edible and small, a perfectly sized treat—and he was famished. "We'll talk tomorrow."

"Tomorrow works for me," Cleo lied agreeably, and ignored the little shiver that snaked down her spine.

And then he was prowling toward her, that dark, sexy gleam in his gaze that still made her breath catch in delicious anticipation. Her heart didn't know she hated him—

or that she knew she *should* hate him. It only beat, slow and hard, the closer he came.

The hotel suite they stood in was a celebration of old-world opulence, a marvel of restoration and generations of money sunk into every detail, and still it faded next to the carnal menace of Khaled. He'd rid himself of his jacket and the shirt beneath it, and as he stalked toward her he was arresting and bold, all that golden skin and the mouthwatering display of his powerful muscles beneath.

If he was less beautiful, Cleo wondered, would that make this any easier? She couldn't tell.

He stopped in front of her, his gray eyes too dark and his dangerous mouth in that grim line that worked through her like sadness.

"Kiss me," he ordered her, and there was something in the way he said it. Something too much like despair. It made Cleo's throat feel tight. It made her clench her whole body, even the soft, hot core of her, where he'd licked her to delirious insanity only a few hours before.

"Khaled..."

But she didn't know what she meant to say. What she could say. He'd given her exactly one way to live in his world and she didn't want to do it. She *couldn't* do it.

"Cleo." It was a whisper. Complicated and dark, and that aching in his gaze that made her tremble. His mouth crooked slightly to one side as he reached over and brushed her cheeks gently before holding her there, hands cupped around her face. "Obey me."

Obey. That terrible word.

And yet it was the only thing she wanted to do, just then. So Cleo ignored everything inside her that railed against him, tilted her mouth toward his and kissed him.

With all of her pain, her regret. The dreams she'd entertained of the life they should have led, her confusion and her worry and that deep, rich vein of anger that ran

beneath it. She kissed him for forgiveness and she kissed
him in accusation, and he held her face in his hard, hard
hands and kissed her back.

As if they had all the time in the world.

It was almost as if he knew this would be the last time.
He sank his fingers into her hair, ignoring the combs that
fell and the way it all toppled down, tugging her even
closer to his heat. It was drugging and dark, utterly perfect, and Cleo couldn't help herself.

She wrapped her arms around his neck and held on
while he peeled the silver gown down, then kicked it aside
when it was at her feet. And she gasped against that delec-
tably hard line of his mouth when he hoisted her up against
him, then pulled her legs around his waist.

He was so strong. Built like steel and all of his power
focused so intently on her. On the wet heat of her, pressed
so intimately against him. On kissing her, again and again,
as if he would never tire of her taste.

His hands brushed that ruinous fire over her skin, his
mouth against her neck made her cry out his name, and
only when she was writhing out her pleasure against him—
mindless and delirious and entirely his—did he carry her
over to the sofa that stretched across the living area.

And then, when he was stretched out above her, Khaled
stopped playing around.

He was relentless. He took her again and again, making
her boneless and blissful against him, so gloriously wrung
out she thought he must know what she had planned. That
the dark, driving need that had ridden him all night must
be suspicion—

But he only took her into the shower in his same grimly
possessive way and washed her, treating her like a piece of
delicate glass. Treating her like something precious—*but
that means nothing to him,* she reminded herself sharply.
I could as easily be a vase. He dried her slowly, using the

great soft towel the way an artist might use paints, until Cleo was finding it hard to keep her eyes from overflowing with all the things she didn't want to feel.

He couldn't be tender. He couldn't be affectionate. Because that was how she'd imagined him for so long in her mind, how she'd told herself he'd be if she only gave him time, and she knew better. Whatever this was, it couldn't be real. *It couldn't.*

She thought he'd reveal himself somehow when he ushered her back out into the bedroom, but he didn't. Khaled simply lay down with her in the hotel bed, then curled around her the way he'd done more often than not in these last, confusing days, holding her close and tight.

As though he loved her, when she knew better.

He doesn't know I'm leaving him, Cleo told herself. *He can't.*

"Settle down," he murmured, a low rumble against her ear, and it didn't help anything to realize that this was probably the last time she'd hear him like this, so close to her he was setting her alight with the furnace of his body, so close she could feel the graze of his mouth against the shell of her ear. He shifted, running one big hand up to rest between her breasts. Holding her there. "Your heart is pounding."

And in the dark, where he couldn't see her, Cleo's eyes filled with tears.

She waited. She kept herself from crying—which she was certain he would notice no matter how drowsy he was—by sheer force of will. The minutes ticked by, and Khaled drifted off to sleep. And soon enough the clock on the nightstand told her it was nearing three o'clock, which meant it was finally time.

This is it, she told herself, oddly paralyzed now that the moment had come. Now that this was actually happening. *It's now or never.*

She told herself that the thing she felt, heavy and bristly and painful, was anything at all but grief.

He didn't wake when she sat up. He didn't even twitch, and still she had to order herself to climb out of the bed and *do* this.

She moved carefully across the floor and crept into the dressing room, closing the door behind her. In the corner stood a selection of wrapped gift boxes, which the odious Margery had selected and Cleo had announced she wanted to inspect personally before they handed them out to Khaled's business associates on this trip. Playing the good wife all the way to the hilt. She'd swapped one of them for her own box back in Jhurat, and that was the one she opened now, expecting to feel nothing but sheer triumph when she pulled out her battered backpack.

Instead, she felt a rush of something far too bittersweet to name.

She shoved it aside and unzipped the pack, dressing quickly. Her favorite jeans, a bit baggier now then she remembered. A long-sleeved T-shirt she knew was comfortable for long trips and a zip-up hooded sweater over it for warmth. Her old Chuck Taylors.

All the emotion that Cleo was fighting so hard to keep at bay swamped her. She screwed her eyes shut, forced herself to breathe past the constriction in her throat, and then she swung the backpack over her shoulders and moved back into the bedroom.

Carefully. Quietly.

Faint light from an outside streetlamp peeked through the drawn curtains, and Khaled lay sprawled in the center of the bed the way he always did, as impressive in sleep as he was awake and aware. As formidably, ruinously beautiful.

More so, perhaps, because it was only when he slept that she could look at him without any mask. Without having to play these terrible games. When she could simply admire him. When he looked softer, more approachable. More hers.

And standing there in the gloom of the late night, dressed like the backpacker nobody she'd been when he'd found her, Cleo stared at him for far too long and wished this wasn't so hard. That it didn't hurt.

How could she have fallen in love with this man?

And why, when he'd made it perfectly clear how little he felt for her and how pathetic her romantic dreams were, hadn't it gone away by now?

He shifted in his sleep then and Cleo froze—certain that her hesitation had ruined everything.

But he didn't wake, and this time, with her heart clattering against her ribs and holding her breath against the fear that she'd lost her only chance to do this, she started for the door and the private elevator that would whisk her away from him.

It was the longest walk of her life.

And when she reached the door, put her hand on the doorknob, she knew.

If she looked at him again, she'd stay. It was that helpless addiction that racked her to her bones. It was that *need* she couldn't seem to banish, even now. If she looked at all at his fierce, proud beauty one more time she'd keep gambling that somehow she could break through to him—and that it was worth trying. She'd keep lying to herself about what this marriage was and lose herself completely in the role she'd taught herself to play for him.

How soon would it cease being an act? How soon would she simply become that perfect, empty shell with none of her inside?

Wanting him wasn't enough. He was the Sultan of Jhurat, and he could replace her. She had no doubt at all that he would—he'd told her that himself. He'd been perfectly, hideously clear. It was long past time she took him at his word.

Cleo pulled in a very deep breath, then let it out slowly.

She ignored the wetness that spilled over from her eyes and down her cheeks, kept her blurry gaze straight ahead of her, and when she walked out on Khaled bin Aziz, Sultan of Jhurat, she didn't let herself look back.

Khaled didn't think anything of it when he woke to discover that Cleo had left their bed. She did that sometimes, didn't she, he thought with more than a little irritation as he stood beneath the pounding heat of the shower. It was more of that slick, to-the-letter obedience of hers that rubbed like a hair shirt against his skin, leaving him nothing but raw and grim.

And he opted not to seek her out in whatever corner of the grand suite she'd claimed as her own, because he knew what would happen if he did. More of that distracting, opulent firestorm—need and passion and all that rich darkness beneath—that he was half-afraid might kill them both. More proof that all she had to do was touch him and he wasn't in control at all.

Later, he thought as he left the suite. He would deal with the mess he'd made of things—of *her,* of this marriage, of all his plans—later.

He was finally finished with the last of his tedious series of sadly necessary morning meetings—the last with a smug and overly moisturized Manhattan financier he'd disliked on sight—when Nasser pulled him aside in the hotel lobby, his expression uncharacteristically dark, and told him something that should have been impossible.

Cleo was gone. *Missing.* No one had seen her all day.

"Has there been a ransom demand?" Khaled asked at once, already berating himself for failing to take Talaat's multitude of threats more seriously. He kept his voice low, aware that he was standing where anyone could hear him in a hotel lobby mere steps from Vienna's famous Opera House, and there was no need to involve the over-eager press.

"None."

"Signs of a struggle?"

He didn't want to imagine that. He didn't want those harrowing visuals in his head. He didn't know what he'd do if—

But Nasser shook his head. "Nothing like that, as far as we can tell. Her mobile phone and her laptop are the only things missing."

It took a moment for that intense jolt of fear to dissipate. For Khaled to concentrate on what Nasser had said. And it was the laptop that gave Khaled pause. He blinked and considered.

The laptop, which was covered in old stickers for bands he'd never heard of and which she kept in a bright orange sleeve that was most assuredly not appropriate for the sorts of events Cleo appeared at these days. The laptop, which Cleo would have had absolutely no reason to take with her outside the hotel room—and never had, as far as he knew, unless she was taking the rest of her luggage as well. Which meant that any would-be kidnappers would have had to take Cleo *and* break into the hotel room to find that laptop while leaving everything else of value in that room behind—

Unlikely.

Khaled considered the scenario for a moment, looking at every angle, not wanting to admit the possibility that she could have played him. Tricked him. *Impossible.*

"Perhaps my wife has taken a day off."

"From what, Your Excellency?" Nasser's voice was mild, as ever. "Surely her life is an endless holiday."

Khaled glared at him, and the other man had the

grace—or the glimmer of self-preservation—to murmur an apology. Khaled moved away from him, pulling out his own mobile as he walked toward a secluded part of the lobby. Because the perfectly obedient creature he'd had at his side these past few months would never do such a thing.

But that wasn't really Cleo, was it?

Her phone rang once. Then again.

The very notion that Cleo was this devious, this calculating—and this good at it, that she could have spent a night like last night with him and then sneaked out without his having the slightest clue—made his entire body tense in denial.

Denial and then, beneath it, a kick of dark, hot anticipation.

"Hello, Khaled," she said, sounding as she usually did, calm and unruffled. Wherever she was, it was quiet.

"I'm assuming that you cannot have been abducted, then, if you're answering your own phone. Much less killed." He could hear her breathing, and he knew. As surely as if he'd packed her bag for her, hired her a taxi. *He knew.* He had to fight to keep his voice level. "Where are you, Cleo?"

"What does it matter?"

"I find it matters a great deal."

"Then by all means," she suggested, and she didn't sound calm anymore, "replace me."

Khaled let out a breath, not realizing he'd held it. He rubbed a hand over his face, unable to tell if he was furious or empty or some odd, painful combination of both. But all he could see was that smile of hers. The real one he'd missed these past few months. Wide and so bright, it had made him feel alive.

As though he could make choices the way anyone else could.

"Is that what this is?" he asked, amazed at how hard it

was to keep his voice cool. "Petty revenge on your part because you didn't care for something I said? I'd have thought that was beneath you."

"This isn't revenge, Khaled." She laughed, and the sound made Khaled edgy. Like ground glass beneath his feet, in his gut. "That suggests you'd care one way or the other that I've left you. We both know you don't."

Every muscle in his body was tense. Too tense. He gripped his mobile so hard he thought he'd break it, and still, he couldn't say the things he knew he should. The things that collided in the back of his throat, made him ache.

The things he couldn't let himself say out loud, because he knew better. Because she deserved better, loath as he was to admit what that meant: that he should never have taken up with her in the first place. That if she wanted to leave him, no matter what rioted in him in opposition to that thought, he should let her go.

His eyes fell shut, and he hated himself. He hated Jhurat. He hated this mess he'd made with his own hands, his own greed for a woman he never should have met in the first place.

But he didn't say a word.

Cleo was quiet for a moment, waiting, he knew, for him to contradict her. He heard a small sound when he didn't, like her breath let out in a small, sad sigh, and he detested himself even further.

"I'm nothing but ordinary, Khaled." His own words were like a spear straight through him. Gutting him, and the worst part was, she said it so mildly. Almost happily, he'd have thought, were it not for that sharp edge beneath. "You should have no trouble slotting a new one in. No one will notice a difference. Least of all you."

Fury poured through him, black and focused, and that was better. That was familiar.

"If you want to fight with me, Cleo, at least do me the courtesy of doing it in person."

"I tried."

He didn't shout, but it was a close call. *"Once."*

"It left a lasting impression."

Khaled realized he was making a fist, and he dragged his hand through his hair instead. But all he could see was Cleo, who wasn't in front of him. Who wasn't in Vienna at all, as far as he knew. Who had somehow lulled him—*him*—into a false sense of security and then crept out under his nose.

As if he was so uncivilized, so barbaric, that she felt she couldn't tell him she was leaving to his face. He didn't know what moved inside him then, a desperate howling through the emptiness, but he hated it.

"I don't accept this," he warned her, that fury shifting low, into darkness. Into intent.

"You don't have a choice, Khaled. It's not pleasant to discover that, is it?"

"I don't think you've thought this through." He found it difficult to control that bitterness in his voice. Or that dark thing inside him, inexorable as a rising tide. "The paparazzi will hound you. You won't find a moment's peace."

"Better the paparazzi than you." She laughed, but it was an ugly sound. "But we both know you won't follow me."

"Are you so certain of me, then?" he asked.

Khaled didn't know what that was that beat in him, demanding and primitive. He had never known himself less than he did in this moment. He felt precarious and wild, balanced on a cliff above a very deep abyss, and he *didn't want* to let her go. Not like this.

Not ever, that possessive part of him whispered.

"I'm certain you don't care enough about me to bother," she said, and there was that note in her voice then that gave him pause. That sounded far too much like a weathered sort of grief, and he knew that sound. He knew how that felt, how it scraped inside. "This is your pride talking, Khaled."

"And what if you're carrying my child?"

She laughed softly, and it scraped in him, digging in deeper than it should have until it became gouges. Leaving ugly marks in its wake.

"I'm not pregnant. I might have been a fool where you're concerned, right from the very beginning, but I'm not an idiot."

"Cleo—"

"Goodbye, Khaled," she said, and there was a huskiness in her voice then that he wanted to mean something.

But even if it did, she ended the call.

And when Nasser—the only person Khaled could trust with this situation, with the truth about his wife's unexpected disappearance from his side in the middle of their European tour—traced her mobile number, he tracked Cleo all the way to a hotel in Johannesburg, South Africa. Of all places.

"Is there any sign of her?" Khaled asked, his own voice flat. He'd resigned himself to this, but he needed to know where she was. She was his wife no matter where she lived, and she would need his protection.

He was back home in Jhurat, in his empty, echoing palace, made five times its size and ten times as barren by her absence. He was staring out through another window without her, and he told himself what he felt was relief.

That this confusing interlude with her was over. That he could move on with his life according to his original plan.

That he could give himself over to his country as he'd always planned.

"I believe she left you a message, Your Excellency." Nasser coughed. "I'll send you a picture."

When the photo arrived on his mobile, Khaled stared,

his pulse kicking in. Hard, as if he were running flat out into a desert storm.

It was a picture of a completely unremarkable hotel bed, with Cleo's mobile phone sitting in the center of the pristine, untouched bedspread. Next to it, she'd left an open package of what it took him long moments to comprehend were birth control pills.

Her message to him, which better resembled a raised middle finger in the classic American style.

Which was when Khaled understood that this wasn't over.

That he had no intention of letting her go.

CHAPTER EIGHT

"HELLO, CLEO."

Khaled's voice was smooth and dark and deceptively casual. It exploded over Cleo in that split second before she saw him, ripping her open like a red-hot brand against her flesh.

He stepped out from the shadows and back into her life with that same leashed intensity and hair-raising, ruthlessly controlled power of his that had haunted her day and night since she'd walked out on him six weeks ago.

Cleo's heart punched through her chest as she came to an abrupt stop in the middle of the uneven sidewalk on Saint Ann Street. Her stomach slammed to her feet and stayed there, making her feel empty and needy and something frighteningly close to lost.

"It's a nice night for a walk, isn't it?" he asked, in that same mild way that made every single hair on her body prickle into uneasy awareness.

New Orleans's infamous French Quarter was mysterious in the sultry evening, as dark and seductive as the air was dangerous and close, from the cracks in the treacherous sidewalks to the beckoning music pouring out from every building on the tourist-packed streets, and Cleo wanted only to blend in. To disappear, the way she did every night, walking like a ghost in and out of the gritty exuberance all around her.

And now, staring at the man who had reared up before her with a certain terrifying inevitability, his gray eyes a dark storm and a certain satisfaction stamped all over his fiercely beautiful face, she wanted to run.

Again.

You always run, a small voice inside her observed, making her frown. Besides, she had the sneaking suspicion that this time, he'd chase her down before she made it to the end of the block.

"Have you taken to lurking about in alleyways?" she asked instead, and it was a struggle to adopt that cool, unbothered tone. It was a battle to simply stand there beneath the streetlamps while the French Quarter ebbed and swirled around her, as caught in Khaled's grip again as if he held her in his fists—particularly when some rebellious part of her wished he would do just that. "That seems somewhat beneath your great, sultanic dignity, doesn't it? You may have to brush up on your stalker skills. Find an approach that better suits your position." She bowed her head slightly and wasn't *too* sarcastic as she added, "Your Excellency."

Khaled only watched her, that gaze of his so intent it seemed to burn into her, through her. The corner of his mouth kicked up slightly, his only response, and Cleo was appalled—if not surprised—when she felt her own body tip over into that same familiar reaction she recognized from before, instant and treacherous.

Damn it. She felt nervous and silly—and her body still longed for him, powerfully—when she should have felt scared. Intimidated. Angry.

Anything but attracted. Anything but *hungry.*

"What do you want?" she asked quietly, because she didn't want to give him the satisfaction of a stronger response. No matter what her traitorous body happened to be doing at the sight of him.

"Guess," he invited her. Less quietly.

Cleo didn't want to guess. She wanted to turn around and run all the way back to the lovely old mansion in the Garden District that Jessie's friend had agreed to let Cleo stay in, far enough away from Jessie's own condo on Canal Street that, they'd imagined, they'd have an extra roadblock in place should Khaled come looking for her.

Cleo had assured Jessie that he wouldn't.

Yet now that he was standing in front of her, she understood that deep down, she'd known this was all on borrowed time. This small and cozy little life she'd built for herself in these past few weeks, her mornings sitting in a bustling, trendy café on Magazine Street pretending she fit into the life all around her, her afternoons and evenings spent taking long, brooding walks around the hectic, frantic, beating heart of this old, battered survivor of a city while she told herself she belonged here.

Deep down, she'd been waiting for him, and she really didn't want to face what that meant.

And he was even better than she remembered, so overwhelmingly *male,* so ferocious, drenched in his absolute authority and that air of command he wore like his own skin. The punch of him against the sweet Southern night was almost too much to take in. He was dressed in dark trousers and one of those soft-as-a-caress shirts of his that managed to cling to every single muscle on his solid, lean chest, and he should have looked like one more tourist cluttering up the busy neighborhood, indistinguishable from the rest.

But this was Khaled. He didn't *blend.* His gray gaze was too direct, too commanding. Too knowing. Even the way he stood before her was a symphony of athletic grace and that carnal menace, like the ruler he was, well used to deference and respect. *And obedience,* that little voice inside of her reminded her. His dark brows rose as he studied her, as if he expected all of that from her, too. Now.

He was in for a surprise, then.

"It's been a long six weeks," Cleo said, and she made no particular attempt to modify that edge in her voice.

"It certainly has."

She ignored that, the silken ferocity of it, the hint of his harsh temper, barely restrained. "I've had a lot of time to get in touch with my anger."

"*Your* anger? Did someone leave *you* under cover of dark?"

If she hadn't been looking right at him, she might have believed that soft, polite tone of his. But she could see the flash of temper in those eyes of his, the way his hard mouth tightened.

She told herself she didn't care, because she shouldn't.

"You don't seem surprised to see me," he said, shifting slightly, so that his shoulders blocked out the whole of the street. Possibly the world.

Cleo shrugged. "You strike me as the kind of man who doesn't like it when his toys go missing, even if he's sick of playing with them." Her reward for that barb was the faint clenching of his jaw, the further narrowing of that implacable steel gaze. "Even if he has no intention of doing anything with those toys except locking them away somewhere. Barefoot and pregnant, if possible."

"Let's step away from the toy box metaphor, shall we?" He used that mild tone that was Khaled at his most lethal, and his gaze was cold, to underscore it.

"I wasn't aware I was being metaphoric," Cleo retorted as if she were unaffected by him. "But I'm not surprised you're here. This feels so tediously inevitable it might as well be déjà vu."

She didn't like the smile that moved over his hard mouth

then, however briefly. Mostly because it rang in her like some kind of bell, and she despaired of herself.

"You are the wife of the Sultan of Jhurat," he observed. "Tediously inevitable though it may be."

"Technically," she said thinly. "And temporarily."

His glare silenced her. "You are famous the world over, Cleo, as you are very well aware—so famous that magazines are sold on the barest speculation that a tight-fitting dress you wear to lunch might in fact be an indication of impending motherhood. Did you not tell me so yourself? There is no undoing it now."

He didn't seem to require an answer and he moved then, prowling around her in a circle that probably appeared lazy but *felt* like a tightening noose, making her itch to break and face him while he did it—but Cleo made herself stand still. She waited.

And she doubted very much that it was an accident that he was doing the very same thing he'd done to her the day they'd met on that side street in Jhurat.

"And yet you wander a notoriously dangerous city in the dark of night, alone. Vulnerable. Wide open to any and all attacks. Advertising to all and sundry your isolation, whether they come at you with a camera or a fist. Almost as if you are deliberately tempting fate."

He completed his circuit and Cleo hated that as she stared back at him, filled with a bravado she hoped he couldn't see beneath to that awful trembling within, she wanted nothing more than to reach out and touch him. To assure herself that this was real, that he was here, that this wasn't that painful dream she had almost every night, swollen with regret and grief, longing and loss.

And she still didn't know when this had happened. She'd thought leaving him would set her free and instead she'd discovered that she'd left her heart behind in his keeping. It made her angry—and anger was good, she told herself. It hid all the pain and uncertainty beneath. It felt like *action*.

"Come on, Khaled." She hardly recognized her own voice, it was so mocking. As if she was someone else—someone as implacably fierce as he was. "Say your usual horrible things about what a disappointment I am and how I could never measure up to your exalted standards and impeccable breeding, or how will I recognize you?"

She was sure she only imagined that flicker of something darker in his gaze, something shockingly like regret.

"It is your reckless disregard for your own safety that concerns me."

"I was perfectly safe," she informed him. "Until now."

"I am a danger to you, that is certain," he agreed, all of that dark heat and hunger, temper and control in that low voice of his, and it made goose bumps prickle down the length of her arms. "But you are a beloved icon, whether you like it or not. Do you know what it would do to my people to lose you?"

"Your people." Of course. This wasn't about him, her, them. It never was. "I didn't ask to be an icon, Khaled."

"Didn't you?" Silken threat, and something agonized beneath it that she didn't want to acknowledge. "But this is about responsibilities, Cleo. Not our little fantasies of the lives we might have had were we different people." He let out a sound that was not quite a laugh, and he never shifted that dark gaze from hers. "You wanted something bigger, did you not? You wanted something other than your small life. Guess what? Bigger lives go hand in hand with far bigger consequences."

For a moment, Cleo couldn't breathe. She remembered sitting in that parlor with him, so long ago, but it was like remembering a movie. Of a very silly girl who should have known better than to think that the lion perched in the chair beside her would do anything but eat her whole.

"I can see the virtue in a tiny little life these days," she threw at him, her voice rougher than she would have liked, because it gave away too much. "I want one."

"And yet you have not returned to the one you left behind in Ohio," he pointed out, the words like a series of blows she had to fight not to crumble beneath. "The one you told me was such a good life. Why not, Cleo? Why spend six weeks in purgatory instead? You could have the entire life you walked away from. You must know this. And yet you are here."

"You don't know anything about my life in Ohio. I doubt you've ever been to Ohio." She sounded too fast, too furious, as though he'd ripped her wide open—but of course he hadn't. He didn't know anything about a small, boring life. How could he? "And I'm not going back to Jhurat with you."

"You seem certain of that, as you are certain of so many things." His gaze was hard and nearly silver in the darkness, and she still wanted to reach over and touch him. So much so, her hands ached with the struggle to keep them to herself. She was horrified with herself. "I am less certain."

"I want a divorce."

That corner of his mouth twitched, but only slightly. "You can't have one."

"I wasn't asking your permission," she snapped at him. "I was announcing a plan of action that has nothing to do with you."

"And yet I regret to remind you that you require my permission to dissolve our marriage, Cleo," he said as if it didn't matter to him one way or the other. It burned in her like acid that she had no idea if it did. "We were married under the laws of the Sultanate of Jhurat. And guess who makes those laws?"

Jessie had cautioned her that this might happen. That Khaled was the kind of man who didn't like to lose. That there would be loopholes within loopholes, and none in her favor.

"Then I hope you're prepared for a very lengthy, very public, no doubt supremely embarrassing separation," Cleo said. "Which will include me walking wherever I damn please. And without the assistance of one of your PR harpies like that Margery."

Khaled blew out a breath, turning his head away and then shoving his hands into his pockets. Hard, as though he'd wanted to do something else with them entirely. He said something she had to strain to hear—but then the thick, seductive darkness was split open by the bright clamor of a jazz trombone and an accompanying trumpet in the nearby intersection, the jaunty notes breaking through the night and echoing off the walls around them as the musicians whirled by in a cloud of vibrant noise.

When they'd passed, when Cleo could breathe again, her heart was making its own kind of clatter and Khaled was watching her, something brooding and yet much too inviting in his dark gray eyes.

"Are your men surrounding me?" she asked, raising her chin as if she might try to fight them off herself. "Am I five seconds away from being thrown in the back of a dark-windowed SUV and smuggled out of the country against my will?"

"It is, I think, high time you watched a better class of film." Khaled's voice was dry, and she didn't want to feel that easing inside her at this unwelcome reminder that he wasn't always so harsh. That he was sometimes even funny. "I have no intention of smuggling you anywhere. This is life, Cleo, not an American action hero franchise." He studied her. "And besides, I think we both know there is no need for such theatrics when all I need to do is touch you and you'd follow me anywhere."

That he was probably right sat like a stone in her, but

she scowled at him anyway and hoped he couldn't see the flush of heat that enveloped her.

"Yes, of course," she said in a bored tone that hurt to produce. "Because I'm so stupid and inexperienced next to—" she waved her hand at him in a gesture that could only be deemed flippant "—all *that*. I don't know that I'd brag about that if I were you, Khaled. But to each his own."

He looked incredulous and thunderous at once. But Cleo just wanted him gone. She wanted this over.

Didn't she?

"I might have let you go," he said softly, but with that dark steel beneath that seemed to slice right through her and lodge somewhere inside her at the same time. "It was what you wanted, what you went to great lengths to secure, and I was not, I am aware, at all the husband you fantasized I might be."

"It had nothing to do with fantasy!" That stung.

"It had everything to do with fantasy," he retorted, and there was a crack in that iron control of his. She could hear it in his voice and it shook her. "It was the easiest thing in the world to make you fall in love with me—you were halfway there already when I took you back to the palace."

"You are a remarkably cruel man," she said quietly, and somehow she knew it was a direct hit.

"That was a simple truth," he said roughly. "Would you prefer I lie to you, Cleo? Even now?"

"Yes," she lied. "You used to be much better at it."

"Too bad." He eyed her, and a different kind of heat twisted between them then, almost too painful to bear. Cleo didn't know how she managed to hold his gaze. "What exactly did I do to you to make you run like that, as though I was some demon you were so desperate to leave that it required an *escape plan?*"

There was absolutely no reason at all that she should feel that bright curl of shame inside her then. She felt it hot and red at the tops of her ears, and the fire of it in her belly. As if *she* were the one who had wronged *him*.

"You know what you did." Her own voice sounded distorted. Choked and strained by all the things she refused to let herself feel.

He was closer then. Too close, she realized, as she started to instinctively back away from him. Cleo forced herself to stand still, no matter how near that put her to that impossibly cut chest of his, that absurdly perfect body. No matter if she could feel the heat of him blasting through her, reminding her how cold it was without him, even here in the soft, warm South.

And no matter that only very dimwitted creatures stood so close to obvious predators like this one.

"And yet here you are," Khaled murmured, a lilt in his voice that arrowed deep into her, making her melt, making another shiver of goose bumps scatter over her skin at the sound. "Happy to remain in the middle of a dark street exchanging barbs with me. Not the faintest shred of fear on your face."

"I'm not afraid of you," she snapped, and the faint gleam in his eyes made her wish she'd curbed that too-revealing burst of temper. Then she thought about what he'd said and she scowled. "And if you *were* going to let me go, why did you change your mind? Let me guess—pride? Arrogance?"

"Yes." That gleam in his gaze intensified, until she could feel it inside her, blazing through all her dark places. "Yours."

She was breathless again, and there was nothing but Khaled, standing too close to her as if they were held in the same vicious grip. As if he knew her far better than she'd imagined he did, and she couldn't believe how stripped naked that made her feel.

"Mine?" she repeated, not sure she wanted to know. But

like everything with Khaled, she couldn't seem to stop. "That's ridiculous."

"The wild-goose chase to Johannesburg was entertaining, of course," Khaled said, his gaze sharpening on hers. "But if you truly wanted to be rid of me, you should have enacted your daring escape without leaving behind that snide little taunt, don't you think?"

"I didn't taunt you."

"Of course you did."

He pulled his hands from his pockets and then he moved, and it was all too smooth, inexorable—and he was there, *right there*. She was up against the wall with his hands flattened on the battered bricks on either side of her head, his face level with hers. And his gray eyes were so dark, so serious, they looked blacker than the thick night surrounding them.

And saw everything.

Cleo shivered, deep inside.

"Why didn't you tell me?"

It was a question, soft against the night. It wasn't an accusation.

She wished it had been. That might have been easier. And she didn't pretend she didn't know exactly what he meant.

"How could I?" she asked, hating that raggedness in her voice. That thickness. "I told you I wasn't ready to have children and you ignored me."

"I don't think so." He kept her pinned to that wall at her back with nothing more than that quiet, implacable stare of his. She was frozen solid, and he wasn't even holding her still. "I tried to keep you in a box, but it never quite worked, did it? You didn't want to tell me because you needed ammunition."

"Ammunition?" Cleo was shaking, though, and she didn't know why. There was something moving inside her, something she suspected he already knew was there, and she didn't want this to happen. She wanted to run. She wanted to hide. But he was *right there,* he was watching her, and she couldn't move at all. There was nowhere left to hide. "Ammunition for what?"

"Proof," he said, in a tone she might have thought was gentle had she not seen that deadly serious look on his face. "How could you possibly stay with a brute like me, a man so controlling you had to sneak your own birth control pills?"

There was a cracking deep inside her, as if the earth were leaping beneath her feet and tearing her apart, and Cleo was lost in it. Torn asunder. A terrible need swept through her, harsh and riotous, and she was drowning in this, in him, in all the things she'd been holding on to all this time—

"That was what *happened!*" Her voice didn't sound like hers at all, and she didn't know she meant to move until she was slapping her palms against the solid, immovable wall of his chest.

"You hid those pills, Cleo," he said in the exact same voice he'd used before, insidious and dangerous and *wrong,* damn him—he was *wrong,* "the same way you hid yourself in plain sight the moment I gave you the excuse. You flaunted your feigned obedience like the thrown gauntlet it was. Because I was your fantasy and you needed an exit strategy and a reason. And you know it."

Cleo was shaking her head, or she was simply shaking, and she couldn't tell which.

"No," she gritted out, desperate and furious and panicked besides. "I loved you. I bent over backward for you. I became a different person for you. I would have done anything for you and you were *horrible* to me that night—"

"Yes," he agreed, and there was that temper there, finally, in his dark, low voice, as if he was losing his own battle with his control. How could she feel that victory? "That *one night* you surprised me and I was mean. Very mean. And your response to that was to act like an ice queen for months and then abandon me without a word." He stopped, as if to catch his breath, but his gaze slammed into her. Spearing through her as though he could hold her aloft with the weight of it alone, and she thought that he could. That he was. "I think perhaps you won that argument after all, Cleo. Given that your love is already in the past tense."

And something inside Cleo simply...snapped. It was like a storm, finally breaking into thunder and frantic sheets of rain. It rolled through her and out of her, and she hardly knew what was left in its wake.

Tears poured down her face, she was sobbing and she found each of her clenched fists held firmly yet gently in his hard, capable hands with no memory of how they got there, his chest tipped against hers so she had no choice but to simply *writhe,* pinned between him and the wall and that raucous tumult that simply would not stop until it wrenched her apart—

"I hate you," she whispered.

It took her a moment to realize that he was far closer to her than he'd been before, and that the insistent drumming she felt and heard wasn't more New Orleans street music but her own pulse. And that it lit her up with every beat. With every breath.

With that look on his gorgeous face, not remote at all now.

"I *hate* you," she said again, desperately.

Cleo had never wanted anything more than for that to be true.

Khaled's beautiful mouth, so hard and so cruel, shifted into that tiny curl that she knew was only and ever hers, and this time she had no doubt that the dark thing she could see in his gray eyes and all across his ruthless face was regret.

Regret and grief and all the rest of the unwieldy things that were tearing her apart where she stood.

"I know you do," he said, gravel and command, and then he leaned forward and claimed her mouth with his.

She was like lightning in his arms, wild and raw and *his,* and she still tasted like fire.

Khaled angled his jaw for that perfect fit, hauling her closer to him, not caring that they were on a public street. Not caring if every last paparazzo found them there and plastered this nearly savage kiss all over the planet. Not caring if the entire world witnessed what happened here.

It was carnal, hot, *perfect.* Unmanageable. Untamable. Intense and *insane.*

It was something more than simply right.

He had planned his vengeance carefully. It had taken longer to locate her than it should have, and he'd found he admired her ingenuity when he wasn't dreaming up ways to make her pay—and dearly—for her temerity.

But then Nasser had taken a harder look at the only friend of hers who *could* have helped her pull something like that escape off. It had taken them no time at all after that to finally locate Cleo herself in a questionable neighborhood in this ruined swamp of a city, made of equal parts jazz and folklore, poverty and grift. And Khaled had come to find her like a righteous thundercloud, prepared to drag her back with him by her hair if necessary.

Where he'd planned to make her pay for her desertion for a very long time to come, in as many highly imaginative ways as he could.

And then he'd seen her.

He'd watched her let herself out of the old house where she was staying, a stately monument to the genteel decay that so marked this humid, flowery place. He'd followed her as she'd walked all over the city with a certain aimlessness and lack of self-preservation that indicated she did it often. He'd noted the slope of her shoulders, the defeated gait in place of her customary grace, how skinny and tired she looked in the uniform of all the women her age in this dirty, grimy, oddly enchanting place: battered jeans and boots, and a flowing sort of sweater wrapped over a T-shirt the color of coffee.

She was his wife. *His* wife. And she looked as though she'd erased him and the life they'd led as easily as she'd left him in the first place.

And yet when he'd stepped out to confront her on this pretty little side street in the middle of the bustle and song of the French Quarter on another long and boisterous night, *vengeance* was the last thing on his mind.

So Khaled kissed her like the drowning man he was.

He kissed her again and again, sliding his hands around to hold her steady for all the ways he needed to taste her, learn her, have her. Remember her. She trembled and she shook, and then she pressed that lithe, amazingly responsive body against him and everything simply *melted*.

And for a long while there was nothing but that white-hot fire, eating them alive, and who cared what was left when it was done.

It was the loud burst of drunken laughter that reminded him where he was, the cackling of the women and loud shoes clomping against the concrete as a group of revelers wandered past. Khaled blinked down at Cleo, unable to believe how out of control things had become.

How out of control *he* had become.

His hands had slid down the back of her jeans and he was cupping that delicious bottom of hers as he held her against his hardness, her silken skin warm and soft against his palms. One of her hands was buried in his hair while the other slid over his naked chest—and he had no memory whatsoever of her unbuttoning his shirt.

He muttered a filthy curse in Arabic, and Cleo's goldsoaked eyes rose to meet his.

"Let go of me," she said, but it was the barest whisper, and he thought he recognized that look on her face then. Pure self-loathing.

"I don't want to," he muttered, but he pulled his hands away anyway.

"Of course you don't," she said, and there was a hard misery in her eyes. "Because you want control. That's all you ever want. You use this *thing* that happens between us to make me crawl, to make me beg, to make me—" She cut herself off, as if she didn't dare speak the words out loud. "On a public street!"

"This *thing* has as much power over me as it does over you," he said through the sand in his throat, that furious clawing inside him again, as though it was new.

Her eyes flashed with disbelief. "I know why you're here, Khaled. This isn't about me. You want to avoid the scandal that happens when the world finds out the fairytale bride has left her fairy-tale prince."

"Three seconds ago we were an inch away from having sex in front of the whole of the city of New Orleans. I obviously don't care that much about a scandal."

"You're the one who built that fairy tale in the first place. Of course you care."

"There's a difference between a marketing campaign and my life," he snapped, that iron control of his a distant memory. "Our life."

"No." Her voice was rough but her chin was high. "There isn't. There never was."

She shuddered, hard, as if she'd been sliced through with a cold wind, and then she shook her head, all that glorious hair of hers swinging slightly as she did, her mouth still slightly swollen from his, and he wanted her in his arms with a fierceness that bordered on sheer desperation.

"Tell me you didn't come here to fetch your wayward wife and shuttle her back home to a life of quiet obedience in Jhurat," she said then, those pretty eyes of serious and dark. "Tell me you came because you actually wanted to talk to me about the things that have happened between us. Tell me, Khaled. I'll believe you."

"Cleo." Her name was like a prayer, and he had given up on praying a long time ago. But he couldn't bring himself to lie to her. Even now.

She shook her head. "That's what I thought."

He wanted to hit something hard, like the wall or the whole damned city itself, but he only stood there before her instead. His shirt hung open, he was disheveled and unhappy, and she was still the only thing he could see. The only thing that mattered.

As though she was the only light in all of this, after all.

"When will you see what this really is?" he threw at her, not caring if he was too loud. Not caring if he knocked down those walls with the force of his voice. Not caring about anything but making sure that she understood this at last. Understood *him*.

"I know exactly what this is."

"You don't. You are the one thing—*this*—" and he moved his hand between them in an inadequate representation of that wildfire that still pulsed in him, in her, in the air around them, thicker and more dense than the Southern night "—is the *only* thing I can't control."

Khaled had spent six weeks without her, in the profoundly dark place she'd left in her wake. He didn't want to do it again.

"You want control?" His voice was a torment, ripped from deep inside of him, and he couldn't begin to imagine what expression he wore on his face when Cleo flinched. But she didn't take her eyes off him.

And Khaled opened up his hands in a heretofore unknown gesture of supplication, and he offered himself to her, right there on a dirty American street surrounded by refuse and drunkards on all sides.

For the first time in his entire life, not the sultan but the man, and he couldn't regret it. If anything, he exulted in it. "Then, by all means, take it. I'll give you all night."

CHAPTER NINE

FOR A MOMENT, CLEO didn't understand him.

She was still fighting off the dizziness from that internal storm that had nearly swept her away, followed by that devastating kiss that had nearly gone too far. As a one-two punch went, it left her breathless and reeling. *Wrecked*.

But Khaled stood there, waiting. Watching her, as if he didn't think she was wrecked at all.

"Exactly what do you mean?" she asked, because she couldn't trust where her mind had gone. Because this was Khaled, who prized obedience above all things—

"Whatever you want," he said, and her temper cracked inside her again, like a whip, lashing into her the way she wished she could lash into him. Because none of this was what she wanted. She'd wanted *happy*. She'd wanted the whole damned fairy tale.

"I don't want to play these games with you, Khaled. We both know you couldn't last five minutes with someone else in control. You'd explode."

"Try me."

His gaze was dark and hard and very, very serious. Cleo's pulse kicked into a higher gear. She ignored it.

"What do you suggest?" she asked in as quelling a tone as she could manage, folding her arms over her chest and hoping she looked tough rather than half-sick with desire and halfway to drunk on all the impossibly steamy images streaming through her head. "Drinking games on Bourbon Street? Truth or dare with all the other tourists who wander past? That sounds right up your alley. You can lecture everyone on your superiority while downing hurricanes and flashing people for Mardi Gras beads."

"Or," he suggested in that low, carelessly seductive way of his, as if he didn't have to *try* to sound that way because he simply *was* that compelling, "you could take the night and do as you like. In private. As I offered."

"You didn't specify private. What you said was *all night*." She tilted her head to one side. "The whole night?"

His eyes gleamed silver and Cleo's mouth went dry when he inclined his head in that impossibly regal, enormously attractive way that meant nothing but bad things for her self-control.

"With me in total control," she clarified, and he held her gaze for a long moment. It took her a beat to realize she was holding her breath.

Khaled nodded again.

"You can't do it," she breathed, but she was already wavering. Imagining.

Plotting.

And Khaled smiled, as if he knew it.

"I can handle it, Cleo. Can you?"

It wasn't until they were both standing in the foyer of the house she'd been staying in, a typical Garden District remodel with its polished wood floors, abundant fireplaces and elegant Southern touches throughout, that it really hit Cleo.

What she was doing. What *he* was doing.

What could happen here, if he was truly willing to let it. If she was willing to accept that the things she felt for him weren't going anywhere.

"And what happens if I simply use you and throw you

out the door tomorrow morning?" she asked him, breaking that simmering silence that had been wrapped around them since they'd left the French Quarter. "Like any other regrettable one-night stand?"

He looked even more dangerous then, with that sizzling heat in his dark gaze and that faint ghost of a curve on his mouth. He loomed there in that foyer as if, were he to shrug, he might bust it wide open with the force he exuded from every pore. Every inch of him the sultan, no matter that they were discussing the terms of a surrender she still didn't believe he could make.

But seeing him here was educational. He was *made* to rule over the desert he came from, truly built for it. He belonged there with every sinew and muscle and bone in his tall, commanding body. Those wide-open spaces. That lonely sky, crowded only at night with the faraway stars. Nothing else could possibly contain him.

Certainly not an overly fussy foyer in a small Southern mansion, filled with cut flowers and darling vases Khaled looked as though he could shatter with his thoughts alone.

"Ah, yes," he murmured, snapping her back to this minefield they were standing in. "Your extensive knowledge and experience with one-night stands. It had somehow slipped my mind."

"For all you know, I've had one every night since I left you." He didn't look particularly concerned with that possibility, which, perversely, Cleo found insulting. "I have you to thank for awakening me to the joys of insatiable desire, after all." She smirked. "Thank you, Khaled."

That dark, narrow gaze of his invited her to keep going, to push him further and who knew where they'd end up— and Cleo's pulse went erratic and much too fast and she could have sworn he knew it.

"You're welcome" was all he said.

"You could at least pretend to be outraged at the very

idea. Break something in a jealous rage. Say something obnoxious and faintly medieval."

It occurred to her after she stopped speaking that she'd as good as admitted she'd done nothing of the sort.

"I would be more than outraged if I thought it was possible," he replied silkily. "I would long to tear every one of your lovers apart with my hands and take out my darker feelings on your sweet flesh. But you didn't touch anyone."

Cleo couldn't tell if she was stung or touched by that. "You can't possibly know if I did or didn't."

"I know you." The way he looked at her then was more powerful than a touch. Darker and deeper. Searing straight through her. "And for better or worse, despite your own preference I expect, you see nothing but me."

She jerked as if he'd slapped her, then felt something hot and breathless spread through her. Leaving her flushed and much too close to wrecked all over again. And Khaled only watched her, as if he could see every tiny thing that happened inside her. Where had that serene mask of hers gone? How had she managed to keep it up for so long?

"I liked the fantasy," she whispered, more to herself than to him. "You were incidental."

But he was the Sultan of Jhurat. He laughed.

"You have accused me of a number of things tonight," he said after a moment, walking farther into the house, his footsteps as loud as her own heart against the gleaming floors. He eyed the prissy living room to his left, then turned back toward her. Cleo realized then that she was still anchored to the floor in the foyer as if she'd become part of the antebellum furniture. "Think of this as your chance to use all those weapons against me."

"This isn't a war." She eyed him, and reminded herself that she'd been brave enough to leave him. She could do this, too. "This is nothing more than sex. This has always been nothing more than sex, dressed up in your *marketing campaign*."

She sensed his impatience more than saw it, and then he crossed his powerful arms over his chest. He'd never bothered to rebutton his shirt and so it simply hung open, that remarkable torso of his *right there*. It made it difficult to think.

"Sex is the symptom, perhaps," he said in his gravelly way that lit a fire low in her belly. "But I think you know perfectly well it's not the disease."

"You called it a disease, not me. Remember that."

"I remember everything." And like that, he was all steel and menace, seeming to loom over her from across the room. "Everything, little one."

"Don't call me that."

But it wasn't because it was a condescending term, used only to put her in her place—which was what she'd told herself over all these long weeks as she'd tried to *think* Khaled out of her system. It was because, despite everything, she loved it when he called her that, as he had in the oasis. Something inside her flipped over and thrilled to it. It made her feel cherished. Precious to him.

She could hate him for that lie alone.

"As you command," he said, with only the faintest mocking edge to his voice.

"Fine," she said. "Let's do this." She roamed toward him with her arms crossed in front of her, only realizing as she drew closer that she was unconsciously mimicking his posture. Because he was the most commanding person she'd ever met, she thought darkly, and gritted her teeth. "Strip."

His perfect brows, dark and naturally arched, rose.

"I beg your pardon?"

"You heard me."

"How deliciously uncivilized, Cleo." His voice was sinful, dark and bittersweet, and she thought she could easily have lost her way in it if the perfect plan hadn't come to her then. "I didn't know you had it in you."

"Don't make me tell you again," she said boldly, and pretended she didn't hear his low laugh.

And then he did what she'd told him to do.

Khaled held her gaze, direct and demanding even while he was the one following orders. He shrugged out of his shirt, letting it fall to the floor behind him in a simple move that called even more attention to the sheer masculine beauty of that chest of his, all of those flat planes and delicious ridges that she knew entirely too well.

And still wanted to taste, so much so that her mouth watered at the thought.

His hands moved to the waistband of his trousers and he maintained that simmering eye contact as he unbuttoned himself. He paused to kick off his shoes and then he thrust his trousers and the boxer briefs beneath to the floor in a single smooth motion.

And then Khaled was perfectly naked, standing there before her, and he didn't look the slightest bit diminished.

It was Cleo who felt off balance.

"Excellent," she said breezily, as if she often had naked sultans at her disposal, ready to leap at her every command. She walked past him with all the false confidence she could summon, heading for the flight of stairs at the back of the house and the master bedroom above. "Follow me."

But she'd forgotten he moved like the night, so quietly she had to keep checking behind her to make sure he was there—following her with that narrow, hungry look on his fierce face and all that fire in his eyes—and she was all too aware that doing so did not exactly emphasize her position of command.

She strode into the master bedroom and then stopped dead in the middle, because she'd underestimated the effect it would have on her to bring him here. The bedroom was done in calming pastels and soft creams, and Khaled in the middle of that was…anything but soothing. He was far too male. Overwhelming. Too powerful to be anything but in charge, no matter what games they were playing tonight, and Cleo wasn't sure what that tiny fluttery thing was, down deep inside her, that wanted to call this off. That wanted simply to throw herself at him and see what happened.

But she already knew what would happen.

Cleo knew she couldn't do that, or this really would be a one-night stand. Their last-night stand, and she accepted, standing there in a stranger's bedroom with this dangerous creature who was her husband, that even though she'd left him that wasn't what she wanted. It never had been.

Khaled studied her for a moment, the faintest hint of amusement on his face, and then looked around. At the graceful two-sided fireplace that dominated the far wall and led into the vast bathroom. At the French doors that opened out over a cozy balcony with only the lush garden below.

Not, she noticed, at the bed that waited there in the middle of the room, as if it hardly signified. As if, unlike her, he didn't have one flaming hot image after another hurtling through his head and making it difficult to stand still. Or breathe.

"I know you think this is all about sex, but you could be in for a surprise," she blurted out, as much to get herself under control as to focus his attention. "What if what I want is you performing acts of service in the nude, like a very large trained dog?"

He took a long time to look back at her, and when he did, she hardly recognized that light in his eyes. Pure, untempered laughter? But that was impossible. This was Khaled.

Though it warmed her in ways she hadn't thought possible to see it. Worse, it made that small, unruly thing inside her chest swell.

"By all means, enjoy yourself thoroughly," he said, and that same current ran beneath his words. It had to be laughter—and it was like a revelation. A bright hot wanting that sneaked into her bones and settled there. Like hope. "Demean me however you choose, if you feel you must. But there are always consequences, Cleo. You know that."

She frowned. "I thought this was a gift. I thought you were surrendering yourself. You can't retaliate for something *you* decided to do."

"Can't I?"

And it didn't matter that he was naked and she was clothed then. He stared at her until she flushed too hot, and then was perilously close to a guilt she refused to let herself feel.

"Don't pretend that should have some special resonance for me," she hissed at him. "It doesn't. I left because I *had* to leave. It isn't the same thing."

"If you say so." But he didn't stop looking at her like that, as if he saw everything. As if he knew things about her that Cleo herself didn't know, and she couldn't tell, any longer, if she hated that or craved it. Or even if it mattered anymore. "You have all the power, Cleo."

"If you dare tell me I always did…" She couldn't finish the sentence, and she was horrified to realize that she was shaking, and that that burning sensation in her eyes was the threat of tears. "You know that's not true. You went out of your way to make sure it couldn't be true."

His dark eyes flashed. "I never said I wasn't a bastard. I only point out that you were never as helpless as you pretend. You've always had control over me, Cleo. You simply never exercised it."

"Because you never *let*—"

She cut herself off when he merely raised that aristocratic brow of his.

"On the bed," she snapped. "Now."

And that time, he really did laugh. At her, but it was still so beautiful it very nearly hurt. It poured over her like sunlight and Cleo wanted nothing more than to make certain he laughed again. Often. Always—

But that wasn't why they were here.

She'd had the courage to leave him. She supposed, in a way, he'd given her that. If he'd never been so certain she could play the role of his wife, she never would have found it in her to imagine she could either—much less imagine they ought to have been more than the narrow little relationship he'd wanted. It was *that* Cleo who'd walked away from him.

She'd had six weeks to figure out that this wasn't a change of clothes, this version of herself. This was who she was. And whatever happened next, whatever became of her battered little heart, she'd earned the person she'd become.

This was her opportunity to prove it.

He took his time walking over to the bed and stretching out on the colorful comforter. Cleo watched him, admiring the play of all that sculpted muscle, the sheer beauty of so much masculine perfection right there before her. Then, when she saw he was watching her, his amusement still so bright in that gray gaze of his, she pulled in a deep breath and started moving.

First she went to the chest of drawers that stood opposite the bed. She rummaged around in the top drawer and pulled out what she wanted—an old pair of panty hose and a light summer scarf. She carried both over to the bed and smiled down at Khaled, pretending she wasn't seriously tempted to forget this half-cocked plan of hers and simply melt all over him.

"Losing your nerve?" he asked her, a quiet taunt that

proved he really could read her. She decided to view that as a positive thing.

"Not at all." She nodded toward the wrought-iron head-board above him. "Grab hold of that."

He shifted, something she couldn't quite interpret moving over his arresting face, but he reached above him and grabbed on to the iron as she'd requested.

Cleo pulled the length of the scarf taut between her hands and leaned in close, fastening his strong wrist to the dramatic curl of iron nearest it. Khaled's other hand came up and grabbed hold of her high up on her side, his fingers just brushing the lower slope of one breast.

Her hastily indrawn breath was much too loud in the quiet of the room, and she had no doubt that he could *see* how fast and hard her heart was beating in the crook of her neck. That he could feel that instant fire in her, radiating out from the simple touch, making her burn everywhere, the way she always did.

She looked down. His dark eyes were glittering. His mouth moved—but he didn't say anything, and she had the impression, somehow, that it cost him.

"Khaled," she said softly, her gaze fast on his. Challenging, even. "Obey."

He thought it might kill him. *She* might kill him.

Cleo was soft and close, leaning against him, her honey-colored eyes defiant and demanding, that distracting mouth of hers within reach—

But he was a man of his word, for all the good it had ever done him. He reached up and grabbed the headboard again, and then he lay there in what passed for obedience when every part of him was tense and hard, and let this tiny little woman tie him to her bed.

Because she wanted to do it. And he'd agreed to let her do what she liked, like the colossal fool he was.

"I had no idea you were so kinky," he murmured, and she pulled the length of panty hose tight. Too tight.

Then only smiled serenely when he slid a dark look her way.

She shifted back away from him, admiring her handiwork for a moment. "I don't think the faintest hint of bondage really counts as kinky, do you?" She laughed when she saw his expression. "This is the Big Easy, Khaled. The rules are a bit different here."

"And what are these rules, exactly? They seem increasingly opaque."

"The rules are what you said they were. Me in total control. All night long. Without interference from His Excellency, the Sultan of Jhurat. Are you ready?"

He was sure it would kill him, then. Without a doubt. Perhaps that was her goal.

"Do your worst," he invited her, as if he was completely at ease.

He didn't know what he expected her to do, but she only kicked her shoes off and then pulled her knees up beneath her, settling next to him on the bed. And then she looked at him for a very long, uncomfortable moment.

"Is this your worst?" he demanded, with perhaps a touch too much aggression. "Staring at me?"

"You might be in for a long night, Khaled," she said, a faint hint of a smirk on her lovely mouth. "You've been under my control for exactly three minutes and you're already cracking." She eyed him until he sighed in some version of surrender, and then she leaned a little bit closer. "I want to know why."

A faint chill of foreboding moved over Khaled's skin, then settled in his gut. He couldn't keep himself from testing his bonds, though he didn't break them. She watched him do it, and he thought he saw a sadness in her pretty eyes that nearly undid him.

It humbled him, certainly. And that made him lie still. Grit his teeth and take it.

"Why what?" It came out far gruffer than he intended, but she didn't so much as blink.

"What happened between your parents, for a start?"

"You cannot possibly wish to know such ancient history. How can it matter now? My mother is dead and my father doesn't know his own name."

"This isn't a debate, Khaled. Answer me." She scowled at him in that way of hers that always undid him, with its total lack of the usual reverence he commanded. That he had missed so much more than he cared to acknowledge. "Or admit that you can't keep your promise. That you can't let anyone have control over you, ever." She shrugged, and her voice was too casual when she continued. "Between you and me, I don't think you can."

Khaled had never before been so adroitly—or literally—hoisted by his own petard. He couldn't decide if he hated it with every shred of his being or if he wanted nothing more than to throw himself at this woman's feet and beg.

Not that he had the slightest idea how to beg, or what for.

This is madness, a voice inside him declared, but he didn't care. He'd never been anything but desperate where Cleo was concerned. He'd lied to himself from the start— anything to have her, anything to keep her, *anything.*

Even this.

"My parents were madly in love," he said after a moment, and he ordered himself to relax as he spoke. "My mother was a tremendous beauty—a great prize—and my father not only won her tribe's traditional lands when he married her, but her heart in the bargain. It was, by all accounts, a tempestuous and passionate connection as well as a political one."

"She wasn't meek and biddable?" Cleo's face was tellingly devoid of expression. Her arid tone, less so. "Quiet and obedient?"

"She was not." Khaled never spoke of these things, and it took him another long moment to pull the different pieces together. To decide how best to tell this tale he didn't wish to share in the first place. "But after she had me, they say, she was never quite the same. Or perhaps there was always that edge in her. It's difficult to know. Her emotions became uncontrollable. Higher highs. Lower lows."

"Did she get help?" Cleo asked in a whisper.

"No, of course not." He eyed her derisively. "My father consigned her to a dungeon and married three younger, prettier wives in rapid succession, forgetting about her entirely in his haste to spread his vicious barbarian seed."

Her scowl returned. Deepened. "A simple 'yes, she got help' would have sufficed."

"And destroy all your dark fantasies about men like me and my father? I would hate to ruin these desperate imaginings for you, Cleo."

"If you don't want to tell me this story, then don't." The color was high on her soft cheeks, but that didn't keep her from aiming that withering glare at him until he felt it like her hands against his skin. "But we'll both know that you used a diversionary tactic to get out of keeping your promises. I'm all right with that if you are, Khaled. I *expect* that."

"My father was in love with her," Khaled said shortly. "He did everything he could. But he was also the sultan, and it was not a stable time in the region. In the end, he was neither the husband she wanted nor the leader the country deserved, and he has spent the bulk of his life torn between the two."

"That's why he shut down the borders," Cleo said after a moment. "For her."

"Yes." Khaled shrugged. "To contain his responsibilities—to focus. But it didn't work. My mother had Amira—and there are a hundred sad reasons why I am twenty years older than my sister, Cleo. My mother spent those years in varying degrees of despair." He met her gaze then and didn't try to hide the grief in his own. For the past, but also for the two of them. "And we all learned far too well that love does not solve anything. It makes things worse. It creates unrealistic expectations on all sides."

Cleo didn't speak. She reached out a hand and put it on his chest, like a boon. A gift. As if she wanted to share these grim memories with him, or help carry the load of them.

A simple little touch, and yet he felt it everywhere.

"After Amira was born, my mother no longer got out of her bed," he continued, not recognizing himself in that moment, lost somewhere between these harsh truths and that warm, reassuring press of her hand against his flesh. "It took years, but she eventually died. The doctors called it a wasting disease, though they couldn't determine any actual cause. But she told anyone who would listen that my father chose his country over his wife, and that was what destroyed her."

Cleo let out a soft breath, and Khaled found he was even more tense than before.

"Did he?" she asked, as he supposed he knew she would, her gaze never wavering from his.

"How can I answer that?" His voice was huskier than it should have been, and there was too much in the air between them. Too much, too tight, too complicated. "He never had any choice but to rule. What should he have done? Thrown the country into the hands of the wicked or the greedy so he could be at his wife's beck and call as she wanted him to do? What kind of man would that have made him?"

"There are compromises, Khaled. There are always compromises."

Her eyes were wide and slicked with emotion and neither one of them was pretending that this conversation was about the past.

"Is this evidence of compromise?" he demanded then. "You running away from me in the middle of the night, then tying me to a bed so you can pry into my history? Where is the compromise in that?"

"Your mother sounds like she was unwell," Cleo said, though her voice was rough and there was that bright gleam in her gaze that spoke of tears unshed. That heavy, aching thing that he felt, too.

"There are words for it these days," Khaled said quietly, as if that might stem the rising tide in him. As if anything could. "But all I saw were two parents who used *love* as their primary weapon against each other. As a battering ram, Cleo. Neither one of them could stop. And they ended up hating each other."

She was silent for a long while. So long he realized he could hear the hum of air-conditioning units from somewhere outside, and the dappled, happy burble of what must have been a nearby fountain. All of that and his own heart, pounding too hard. Reminding him why he never, ever discussed this.

Tearing him apart with every jarring thud.

"So this is what you took from that story?" she asked, when he had begun to think she might not speak again.

"Not 'that story.'" His tone was curt. "My life."

"That the mistake—the tragedy—was your parents' loving each other. That's what you decided."

He might have gone scathing then, but she sounded so much more tentative than she had before, as though she was trying her hardest to figure him out. Khaled thought he should have told her not to bother with such a fool's errand, but he couldn't deny that he liked it, all the same. It made him soften slightly.

"I decided that no wife I ever took would mistake the matter," he told her, far more gently than he might have. "That there would never be any doubt. I am the sultan and I, too, must rule Jhurat whether I like it or not."

She didn't look away. Her chin rose. "You're trying very hard not to say that you will always choose your country first."

He was. Damn her.

"It's not that simple." But he couldn't lie to her. It occurred to him then that he'd never been able to lie to her—and all of this would have been so much easier if he could have. He shoved that odd notion aside. "But yes. I will always choose Jhurat. I must. And yet, Cleo, here I lie. Lashed ineptly to an iron bed a planet away from where I should be tonight. So perhaps none of these choices are as black-and-white as you'd like to believe."

"But it's more than that." She shifted, and as she sat back he found he could only marvel at how pretty she was. That it broke through all the rest of this like the sun on an overcast day, and he had no idea how he'd become so weak where she was concerned. So enamored. Or why he missed the soft weight of her hand so terribly it made him tense with the loss. "You told me I had to adhere to a very strict role. That I had to *obey*."

"I was trying to protect you," he grated at her, only dimly aware that he'd clenched his bound hands into fists. "My mother spent her life feeling abandoned and discarded and alone. If you never expected anything of me, how could you feel those things?"

Her face registered astonishment. "Are you— You're saying that was for my own good? You can't be."

"I wanted to protect you."

"By humiliating me as I knelt before you, naked." He'd

never heard a tone quite so withering. "By keeping me at arm's length by day and only coming to me at night, as if there was something wrong with me."

Khaled glared at her. "I wanted you to fall, but not that far. I wanted to keep you safe."

"Then why did you work so hard to make me fall in love with you?" She shook her head when he started to protest. "You know you did. Why did you spend that week with me in the oasis? How was that anything but...too many expectations?"

"Because when it comes to you, Cleo, I find that nothing goes according to plan." He indicated his bound wrists. "Including this."

And then he decided he was done with this game. That it was time to finish this, once and for all. He gave the ties that bound him a quick jerk, and was free.

CHAPTER TEN

CLEO HARDLY HAD time to register that Khaled was moving when he simply pulled her to him, then rolled so she was beneath him. By the time she understood what was happening, Khaled had balanced his weight on his elbows and was holding her head in his hands, his fingers spearing deep into her hair.

"You promised," she whispered.

"I am a terrible man, Cleo," he told her, his gaze so dark she trembled. "A selfish monster from the very beginning. And nothing I ever think I ought to do with you seems to work. Wasn't that the point of this exercise?"

She was shaking. "You were only *pretending*. You could have broken free at any time!"

"Perhaps, then, you should ask yourself why I didn't choose to do exactly that."

He didn't wait for her to answer, didn't pause at all, he simply leaned forward and kissed her.

And it was unlike anything that had come before.

That searing, intoxicating current of passion was there, as it was always there, simmering deep within and informing everything, but this time, Khaled's kiss was sweet. Shattering. Something like sacred.

His mouth moved over hers like a revelation. Like some kind of quiet song that Cleo felt inside her, each exquisite note washing over her like the purest light. Quiet and bright.

Perfect.

Cleo clung to him, transported. Feeling strangely hushed and torn wide open at the same time. Her heart felt too big for her chest, and she felt all the confusion she'd been trying to keep locked away inside her spill over and trickle from her eyes.

And this time, she didn't care.

He was fully naked and deliciously hard against her belly, and yet he did nothing but kiss her in that same slow, thorough way, as if there was nothing on earth but this. This kiss. This sweet heat. The sheer joy of their mouths meeting, touching, taking them both somewhere that was only, ever, gloriously theirs.

It didn't occur to Cleo to do anything but kiss him back, losing herself utterly. Kissing him until time ceased to have meaning. Lazy and long, as if this kiss was the only thing that could ever matter.

As if Khaled were the only thing in the world, and who cared how fantastically dizzy she was, how wonderfully weak beneath him, their bodies moving as one, tasting, touching, together—

And she was so far gone that she didn't understand when he pulled away. Or why he lifted his head and froze for a long moment, then swore.

She started to ask him, but then she heard it. The overexcited clanging of what could only be the doorbell downstairs.

"Do you know anyone who would drop by at nearly midnight?" Khaled asked her, a rueful look in his eyes, gone nearly silver.

Cleo blinked. "Aside from my many lovers?"

The smile he turned on her then was as astonishing—

and as beautiful—as it was brief. But she hoarded it to her anyway, dazzled.

"Aside from your soon-to-be late minions, yes."

"No. I've never encouraged drop-by visits, to be honest." She smiled back at him. "Also, I only know one person in the entire city of New Orleans, and she has her own key."

The doorbell rang again. Khaled's thumbs moved, stroking down her cheeks, and his eyes went dark as she watched. It fell through her like a change in temperature. Like a sudden shadow across the sun.

"Then that will be for me."

Cleo didn't understand the heaviness in his voice, much less the look on his face as he moved, rolling from her and to his feet in a single lethally smooth motion that mocked even further her attempt to physically restrain him. Had she honestly believed she was holding him against his will? That she could?

He stalked from the room, as unaffected by his lack of clothes as ever, and Cleo trailed him, watching all of that smooth ruthlessness in action as he moved down the stairs like liquid and then pulled on his boxer briefs and trousers with the same swiftness as he'd removed them. Then he went to the door.

"Who is it?" he asked through the heavy wood, sounding surly and dark, and there was absolutely no reason in the world that such a particularly cranky male tone should wrap around Cleo like smoke. She almost laughed at the instant bloom of heat between her legs, the tug on her heart.

And she knew enough Arabic to understand that the man on the other side of the door was part of Khaled's security detail, who, she was suddenly certain, had indeed been circling her earlier, just as she'd imagined.

"Bad American action movies?" she asked him.

Khaled shot her a look over his shoulder and didn't quite

smile, though his eyes gleamed. "I would never have you thrown into one of the SUVs, Cleo. I would escort you into one, like a gentleman."

Cleo was smiling as Khaled let his guard inside, and she stood where she was in the living room as the two men spoke in a quick, intense undertone. Then the other man exited and Khaled stood there for a moment. His head tipped forward and he let out a breath that was much too close to a sigh, and Cleo felt gripped by something fierce. Something with sharp, deep talons that made her wonder that she'd been smiling only moments before.

"I must return to Jhurat," Khaled said, and when he turned to face her he was utterly expressionless.

"Has something happened?" she asked, and she wasn't sure she recognized her own voice. Or the way her hands had become fists and hung there, hard and angry, at her sides.

"Something always happens," Khaled replied in a short tone. "Something always will. But in this case, they think they have Talaat's pissant band of rebels—I refuse to call them an army—pinned down in one of the villages. But the victory will look shallow and invite debate if I am not there to direct it."

He moved as he spoke, and Cleo blinked, realizing only when he reached down to snatch his shirt from the ground that Khaled had never shared matters of state so readily before. Why was he doing it now? And why did it make her feel as if she were standing much too close to the edge of a long, hard fall?

"What if I assert the power I'm supposed to have tonight?" She watched him as she said it. His mouth twisted into something grim. He pulled his shirt on, and yet she had the sense he was waiting. "What if I demand that you stay? To delegate?"

He took a long time buttoning up that shirt, and when

he was finished, he looked at her with his gray eyes like shadows.

"Don't do this."

"This was what we agreed." But she was whispering.

"Cleo." She'd never heard him sound like this. She didn't even know how she'd categorize that rough scrape of his voice. "Do not ask me to choose between my country and my wife. I can't win. And neither can you."

"What if I don't care about winning?" Her voice sounded the same, and she knew what it was then. *Broken.* "What if I want you to stay?"

And Khaled looked haunted. Wrecked, as surely as if she'd torn him apart with her hands. Cleo was hugging herself, her hands still in fists, but she couldn't seem to do anything else but stand there and watch him.

He stamped his feet into his shoes, and the sound was much too loud. Shots, one after the next, and as painful.

Or maybe that was only the taut, dense silence surrounding them.

"I thought what happened upstairs—" She tried again, not even sure what she was grasping for, only aware that she had to. She had to try.

"Yes," he said darkly. "That was an object lesson, Cleo, but not one you want to learn. As you say, I could have broken free of your restraints at any time."

"Then why submit to it in the first place?" she demanded. "Why go to all that trouble to fake it?"

"Because you wanted me there and I didn't want to break free," he said, and there was a helpless kind of grief in his voice then. "But I also do not want to be the kind of man—the kind of sultan—who fails his country. I couldn't live with myself."

"Meaning, you will never choose me." He didn't argue, and she shook her head, hoping that could conceal the way the rest of her shook. "Some vows are more like curses, Khaled. You should think about that."

"I am not cursed." His gaze was a storm. He lifted one hand and pounded it against his chest, the blow loud and hard, though he didn't seem to note it. "I am the Sultan of Jhurat. It is not a title to me, Cleo. It is *who I am*."

"Khaled—"

But she had no idea what she was saying, or when her tears had started to fall again, and it hardly mattered anyway. He wasn't listening. He stood there, so close and yet so remote, and his gaze burned through her until she was nothing but cinders and the salt of her own tears.

"I love you," he said, and it sounded as though it was ripped from him, a dark and troubled confession. "I can't seem to stop, no matter what I do. You hate me when I try to protect you, and the more I'm with you, the less I want to try." He advanced on her, and Cleo stood there and did nothing but watch him come. Helpless. Powerless. As caught by him as if she were still locked away in that bedroom he'd refused to share with her. "But I still must choose my country. I will always have to choose my country. I *am* my country—and we have already established that it will eat you alive." He reached over and dragged a thumb over her mouth, tracing the shape of her lips. "It will drive you insane. And I can't live with that, either, as much as I wish I could."

"Khaled."

He ignored her. And worse, he stepped back, a kind of fury and misery stamped on his fierce face that she felt inside her, a sharp, spiked belt of agony.

"So this? All of this? My love, such as it is?" He laughed, and it was a frozen, bitter sound. It seemed to take up all the air in the room. "It's nothing but selfishness. If I knew what love was, Cleo, I would have let you go. I wouldn't have followed you here. I wouldn't have detained you in the first place, seduced you, married you. You've known that from the start."

He backed away from her, and Cleo was trembling openly now, but Khaled only pressed his lips together in a firm line.

And when he spoke again, his voice was a harsh rasp. A stranger's. Final. "So have I. And I still have to go. I always will."

The heat was a living thing that slammed into Cleo when she stepped off the plane and onto the metal stairs that led down to the private airfield some thirty kilometers outside the old city. And the palace it had been built to contain.

She had to stop and catch her breath, it was so relentless, and then she made her way down to that sun-baked Jhuratan soil, amazed that she felt a solid thump of something like homecoming when her feet hit the ground.

But that was getting ahead of herself, and she knew it.

"My lady, it is a great pleasure indeed to welcome you," said Khaled's head of security from his place some three strides away, while an armored car and driver waited even farther behind him. Nasser inclined his head when she met his gaze.

This was it, Cleo told herself firmly. She was really doing this.

"Are you sure?" Jessie had asked, not making any attempt to hide the dubious note in her voice as she'd watched Cleo pack.

It had been three days after Khaled had left New Orleans. Three days while Cleo beat herself up in that perfectly manicured Garden District house that wasn't in any way her home. Three days while Cleo had faced the unvarnished facts.

She hadn't told a single person besides Jessie that she'd left Khaled in the six weeks she'd spent in New Orleans.

Not her family. Not anyone. If she was honest with herself—finally—she knew it was because she'd been waiting for him to come after her.

Which meant that no matter how much she'd prefer to deny it, she was as manipulative as it sounded like his mother had been in her day. Staging dramatic scenes to force him to choose. Never taking responsibility for her own choices in return. The truth was, as he'd pointed out, she could have gone home to Ohio, but she hadn't. When Cleo had left Brian, she'd never regretted it for an instant. She'd wondered how she'd been so blind, but she'd never wanted him back. She'd traveled for months, which was more or less the precise opposite of *waiting*.

When she'd left Khaled, she'd cried all the way to New Orleans and every night thereafter. She'd tortured herself with dreams of him. His perfect, scalding kiss. His smile. And the moment she decided to return to Jhurat and work on her marriage instead of running from it, she felt nothing but intense relief. She told herself that had to mean something.

"He never pretended to be anything but what and who he is," she'd told Jessie while she zipped up her small suitcase. "I'm the one who wanted him to be some fantasy version of himself."

The one who had been such a child, if she was honest. She'd wanted *happy ever after* above all things, no matter what. She hadn't thought much about what it might take to get there, or even what that really meant. Such as, that it didn't end at the great big fairy-tale wedding—that was where it *started*.

But in order to get there, she had to stop thinking about what she *deserved* and think a whole lot more about what she was willing to *give* instead.

Khaled loved her, she knew he did, yet he was willing to give her up because he thought that would make her happier in the long run. That was what she'd sat with after he'd gone, shaking there in that fussy house all by herself. He'd made her feel beautiful and capable. He'd been trying to protect her in his own terrible way. And what had she done in return?

He'd laid it all out before her on Saint Ann Street and she knew he'd been right, as unpleasant as all those truths were for her to swallow. She'd left him without a word. And then she'd thrown her birth control pills in his face— because on some level, she'd known exactly what that would inspire him to do: come after her. And when he did, she'd made him give more than he'd wanted to give because it was what *she* had wanted. Then, at the end, she'd delivered an ultimatum to cap it all off.

Cleo had come to the lowering conclusion that she was a spoiled brat.

"You know I'll support you no matter what," Jessie had said carefully. "But I feel I wouldn't be any kind of friend to you if I didn't remind you that you were in a panic when you left him. You were convinced that if you stayed with him, you would disappear completely into his life."

"I'm not an innocent in this," Cleo had told her, and there was so much she couldn't—wouldn't—share. She'd shoved a hand through her hair and held it there at the crown of her head. "I think the feeling of disappearing has to do with real compromise, and I'm as bad at is as he is. No wonder I panicked."

Jessie hadn't looked convinced, but she'd nodded. "But do you think that if you go back he'll see that as capitulation?"

"I don't know," Cleo had whispered. "But I love him."

And for the first time, she understood how deep that ran, how true it was, how it had sneaked inside and taken root without her being entirely aware of it. How it filled her from the inside out, and of course that felt like *too much*.

Of course she'd run from it. It felt like his desert sky, enormous and unfathomable, endless and bright.

She'd looked at Jessie helplessly. "I have to go and find out. I have to try."

And it wasn't until Cleo was hours into the long flight back to Jhurat that she'd realized that she'd never tried particularly hard with Brian. She'd certainly never considered trying after she'd found him cheating. Maybe that was why she wasn't worried about *capitulating* now. Because as Khaled had shown her that night he'd let her tie him to her bed, surrender was only a negative thing if it represented a loss. Otherwise, what was it but a little bit of bending?

And love wasn't worth much if it couldn't stand to bend.

The car moved swiftly through the clusters of small sun-beaten villages outside the city walls, and then through the towering gates into the old city itself. Cleo saw the ancient buildings, the spires high above and the bright, colorful stalls cluttering the streets and alleys of the marketplace. She saw the slick new hotels and skyscrapers sparkling next to literal hole-in-the-wall restaurants that looked to date back a thousand years. A hodgepodge of vision and determination next to the inexorable march of history.

Just like Khaled, in his way.

It made a lump grow in her throat.

When the car entered the labyrinthine tangle that marked the area around the palace, she found she was holding her breath. Expecting Khaled to appear, somehow, and stop the car the way he had once before. As if he could bookend this whole thing and make it right by taking charge of it. By taking all the responsibility for everything that happened between them once again.

But he didn't appear and Cleo was forced to face the fact that if she wanted him, she would have to do this herself.

He'd accused her of pride and arrogance, and it was

only now, driving back through the gates of his palace and back into the life she'd run away from, that she understood how true that was.

Remember that I warned you, he'd told her long ago, and she'd ignored him, because it hadn't fit in with her fairy-tale fantasies.

But this time, Cleo didn't want the fairy tale. She didn't want any fantasy.

She wanted her husband.

Khaled didn't turn around when the door to his office opened and then shut, assuming it was one of his secretaries or guards who wandered in and out freely. He ran his hand through his hair, scowling out the window at the city spread out before him and the waiting, watching desert in the distance while he listened with growing irritation as one of his ministers complained. And complained.

"Surely," he interrupted when he could take no more, and he wasn't particularly polite about it, "it is time to count this as a victory." The old man sputtered. "My cousin is in custody and will be enjoying the hospitality of the palace guard until such a time as it is politically useful to release him. Talaat's resistance movement has disappeared without their leader to rouse them into action. It would be difficult for us to be *more* decisive or more successful, would it not?"

He didn't wait for the inevitable spate of further grievances; he simply did himself a favor and ended the call. And didn't move for a long moment.

Jhurat lay before him. His choice. His future. His doom.

And if he felt the loneliness of the desert more keenly than he had before, well, he hoped that time would wear that away the way it did the shifting sands, year after year. Until there was only emptiness and the hint of memories, the wind and the sky. Jhurat would endure. So would he, one way or another.

"Is this what brooding looks like? I've always wondered."

Khaled stiffened. Then wondered if he was adding auditory hallucinations to his collection of issues, marking him as unstable as his father, precisely as Talaat had warned—

But no. He turned slowly, very slowly, and his wife— his beautiful Cleo—was sitting in one of the cumbersome chairs that were pulled up before his desk, looking for all the world as if she'd never left.

And, oh, the things he wanted. The things he needed.

He allowed himself none of it. He only studied her, looking for some clue as to why she'd come here. Drinking in the elegant lines of her face, her body, the sleek riot of her multicolored hair. Ignoring that reckless, leaping thing inside his chest.

"Nothing has changed," he said, breaking the silence when it drew on too long. "In fact, it is worse. I am now wildly popular. It's bad enough to be a mediocre sultan who can't govern efficiently, or so my childhood taught me. But I am a hero now. The demands on my time will be excruciating and never-ending."

"I'm not your mother," she said, and he rocked back on his heels at that. He moved closer to the desk that separated them, then shoved his hands deep in his pockets because he feared they would do his speaking for him.

The truth was, even this quiet, painful little conversation felt like a burst of sweet, refreshing winter cold in the middle of the desert summer. As though she'd brought all the air back into the palace, and he could finally breathe.

But Khaled knew that this time, he had to let her go. Because he wanted so very badly to tie her up, lock her down and make certain she never left his side again. And that very impulse, he knew too well, would kill them both, sooner or later. He'd already tried it.

"Why are you here, Cleo?" he asked quietly. "I thought New Orleans was enough. Have you come to make it harder?"

"I'm not your mother," she said again, and she rose then, that lithe grace of hers calling to him as surely as if she'd shouted at him.

She circled the desk, never taking her eyes off him, and she didn't stop until she was close. Too close. Then she leaned forward and slid her palms along his chest, and it was the sweetest torture Khaled could imagine. He frowned down at her, keeping his own hands firmly planted in his pockets, and pretending he couldn't feel the arching flames of that wildfire that only she called out in him.

Only she could call it. Only she could quench it. And he couldn't permit either. He wasn't sure he'd survive it intact this time. He couldn't take the risk.

"I'm sorry," she whispered, those eyes of hers so wide and serious. "You have no reason to believe me, but I'm not going to do what she did. I'm not going to make you choose—I married *you*. I know who you are, despite what I might have shown you over these past months. But I think I know who I am a little bit better now."

He broke then. He pulled her hands away from his chest and held them in his, unable to stop himself from kissing one, then the other.

"I want to believe you," he managed to say, though his voice was hollow. "But I can't."

"You don't have to believe me right now," she said, and he could see that sheen of intense emotion that made her gaze that much more brilliant. He could feel her trembling, slightly, and it nearly undid him. "I want to try again, Khaled."

He shook his head, and it actually, physically hurt him to do it.

"This won't last, Cleo." She started to speak but he kept going, cutting her off. "I've *watched* this happen. I can't do it again. And especially not if it's you."

"Khaled—"

"I am a profoundly selfish man," he gritted out. "Don't you understand that by now? I don't *want* to resist you. Don't make this harder than it has to be." His gaze searched hers, but that didn't help. And he was hoarse from the battle inside him when he spoke again. "Let me do the right thing."

"This *is* the right thing," she said. She moved then, taking her hands from his and using them to reach up and cup his face. "We are *right*, Khaled. That's why it hurts so much."

"I think that rather proves the opposite."

"All we've shown each other so far is how inflexible we are," she said, and he felt as if all those dark things in him were filling up with her voice, with all that light she spilled all around her so effortlessly. Warmth. Peace. The sweetest honey. He was only a man. He could only take so much. "So now we know the worst. But what if we're not your parents? What if we figure out how to bend instead of break?"

Bend, he thought. That was what was happening inside him now, what had been happening whether he liked it or not since the day they'd met. All of that blackness he'd carried inside him turning over into grays and blues. All of her light chasing out the shadows.

As though forever started right now, if they dared.

"I am the Sultan of Jhurat," he told her, but he found he was smiling, and she was, too. "I do not bend."

"Yes, yes," she said, and rolled her eyes. "You are the great and terrible sultan. The world bends around you."

"I don't care about the world," he told her gruffly, lifting her up against him and vowing then and there that he would never lose her again. Not ever. No matter what happened. No matter what it took, what beds he would be forced to let her tie him to, what *bending* would be required. "It's you I want. I always have."

"I'll do my best to make sure you always will," she told him fiercely.

"Be sure about this," he told her, every inch of him the autocrat. "I won't let you go this time. I really will detain you. Permanently."

"I promise you, Khaled," she whispered, a dark current of need, and that bright light besides, wrapped around him like joy, "I will never give you cause to doubt I love you again."

And right then and there, on the great desk his grandfather had won in a war no one remembered, with Jhurat spread out before them like a stark and beautiful portrait, they started making good on all their promises.

Five years later Cleo lounged lazily in the cool tent at the side of the oasis's crystal-blue waters, and thought they'd kept those promises well.

Khaled walked in from the bright afternoon, the sun seeming to cling to his perfect form an extra moment before her eyes adjusted. And then it was only his brilliance she saw, which he generated all on his own.

"Did it work?" she asked as he dropped down beside her and gathered her to him, kissing his way from her temple to the corner of her mouth.

It still made her shiver.

"It did," he said. "It turns out, I am hypnotic, as I always believed. She dropped off to sleep by the second verse."

He had been gone much longer than that, Cleo knew, tucking their two-year-old in for her afternoon nap.

"And then you watched to make certain she was breathing."

"Of course," he said, and smiled. "And to protect her against any nightmares that might arise. It is no more than my duty."

They'd worked out their own compromises across the years. For every three months in the palace, Cleo insisted they spend a solid week alone in the oasis. She'd learned how not to run or hide. He'd learned how to delegate. They'd both learned how to bend. He had dismissed Margery and others like her and Cleo had made a point to spend more time with Amira who, as she'd once predicted, had left her attitude behind when she'd stopped being a teenage girl.

They tried. Every day, they tried.

And then, when they were both ready, had come their perfect daughter. Gorgeous Amala Faith with dark, flashing eyes like her father, who had wrapped the both of them firmly around her chubby little fists.

But that didn't mean Cleo didn't exult in her nap times, when it was only the two of them again.

"Did you wish to sleep the afternoon away, my love?" Khaled asked, with false sincerity, working his way down her neck until Cleo sighed happily and stretched against him, pressing herself into him in that way that never failed to make her breath catch, even all these years later. "Like our daughter will, God willing?"

"I may have already fallen asleep," she teased him. "From boredom, you understand. Is that what you mean, Your Excellency?"

"Close your eyes, then," Khaled replied, and he looked up at her with that smile he wore so often now. It made him indisputably beautiful, and never quite as remote as he'd been. Never quite as cruel. "I'll try not to disturb you with my tedious attentions."

"What if I don't want to close my eyes?"

"Cleo," he ordered her, that smile of his gone wicked, as surely as she'd gone molten. "Obey."

And Cleo did.

Because *forever* with this man was so much better than any fairy-tale fantasy she could have concocted on her own.

And because every now and again, obedience felt *good*.

* * * * *

MILLS & BOON®

Why shop at millsandboon.co.uk?

Each year, thousands of romance readers find their perfect read at millsandboon.co.uk. That's because we're passionate about bringing you the very best romantic fiction. Here are some of the advantages of shopping at www.millsandboon.co.uk:

* **Get new books first**—you'll be able to buy your favourite books one month before they hit the shops

* **Get exclusive discounts**—you'll also be able to buy our specially created monthly collections, with up to 50% off the RRP

* **Find your favourite authors**—latest news, interviews and new releases for all your favourite authors and series on our website, plus ideas for what to try next

* **Join in**—once you've bought your favourite books, don't forget to register with us to rate, review and join in the discussions

Visit **www.millsandboon.co.uk**
for all this and more today!